Broken Promises

A MARY O'REILLY PARANORMAL MYSTERY

by

Terri Reid

Beware the Jabberwock, my son!
The jaws that bite, the claws that catch!
Beware the Jubjub bird, and shun
The frumious Bandersnatch!

~Lewis Carroll

This book is dedicated to all those who have checked under their beds, closed their closet doors securely, turned out the light and pulled the blankets up high, just in case.

BROKEN PROMISES – A MARY O'REILLY
PARANORMAL MYSTERY

by

Terri Reid

Copyright © 2012 by Terri Reid

The author would like to thank all those who
have contributed to the creation of this book. Richard
Reid, Sarah Reid, Debbie Deutsch, Jan Hinds, Ruth
Ann Mulnix, Lynn Jankiewicz and Liz Solomon.

And especially to the wonderful readers who walk with me through Mary and Bradley's adventures and encourage me along the way. Thank you all!

Prologue

The sky was the soft turquoise that slowly slips into the starry blackness of a spring night. Henry Madison climbed the porch stairs deliberately, leaving a residue of the day's accumulation of dirt and dust from his leather work boots. The spicy sweet scent of lilac drifted on the calm breeze from an overgrown bush next to the porch. He stood in front of the door and inhaled deeply, letting the fragrance fill his lungs and ease the stress of the day. His shoulders sagged slightly and he slowly rolled his neck, closed his eyes and enjoyed the moment of peace. Then he reached forward, grasped the doorknob firmly and let himself into his home.

"Daddy!"

The piercing scream of his seven-year-old daughter, Clarissa, echoed in his ears and blossomed in his heart. He dropped his toolbox on the bench just inside the door and squatted down, waiting for his very own brown-haired, hazel-eyed, human cannonball to hurl herself into his arms. It was his favorite part of the day.

Her tiny body thumped against his chest and she wrapped her arms around his neck, hugging him tightly. He buried his face into her hair, inhaling the scent of baby shampoo and soap.

Her father was her hero. She loved the way his smile crinkled his whole face, even around his eyes. She loved the way he smelled, like wood shavings and fresh air. And she loved the feeling of security she felt once he stepped in the door. Daddy was home, he would take care of everything.

"I missed you so much," she said, and then moved closer and whispered into his ear. "Mommy had a sad day today."

Folding her into his arms, he held her for one more moment, and then he gave her a kiss on her cheek. "Let's go in and see if we can't make Mommy feel better."

He stood, grasped her tiny hand in his and together, the large man and the tiny girl, walked through the house to the small sunroom in the back. The floor was scattered with Legos and it was clear Clarissa had been constructing some kind of architectural masterpiece for her princess collection to live in.

His wife, Becca, was resting on a small couch with a knitted afghan over her legs and a book, faced down, in her lap. She looked up and smiled at him.

She still took his breath away. Even after ten years of marriage, her ethereal beauty, her tranquil smile and her hesitant, almost fearful nature, engendered feelings of love, protectiveness and awe. It was as if he had somehow captured a woodland nymph and brought her to live in man's world.

"How are you feeling today?" he asked, sitting on the corner of the coffee table next to the couch and taking her hands in his.

Meeting his eyes, she shook her head slightly, holding his questioning for a moment. "Clarissa, darling, could you do me a favor and go upstairs and get my pink sweater?" she asked.

Clarissa nodded dutifully. "Okay, Mommy," she responded immediately and raced out of the room.

"She's so grown up," Becca said with regret, "too grown up. She hasn't had much of a chance to be a child."

"She's fine, she's great," Henry argued. "She just loves you and is concerned, like I am. What happened today?"

She tightened her grip on his hands. "He called again today," she said, shaking her head slowly. "He must know about me and he's going to try and take her away."

Henry leaned closer and pulled his wife into his arms, holding her, as he had his daughter only a few minutes before. "Darling, he can't take her," he crooned softly. "She's legally ours. He gave her up. He has no rights to her. Just because you're a little under the weather doesn't change anything. I promise, you don't have to worry about this. You just have to worry about getting better."

She leaned away from him and met his eyes. "He said he was coming to town and he wants to meet with us to convince us to give her up," she explained.

Tenderly caressing her long, blond hair, he guided her back into his arms. "I'll meet with him. I'll go to Sycamore and let him know, in no uncertain terms, that Clarissa is ours and he has no legal rights. And, if he continues to harass us, I'll have a lawyer contact him."

She sprang back from his embrace. "But we can't afford…"

He kissed her forehead. "We won't need to call a lawyer," he reassured her. "All we have to do is threaten and he'll back away. He's a smart man; he knows he doesn't have a legal leg to stand on. He just thinks he can intimidate us."

"But he's a dentist and he has a lot of money," she argued.

"Maybe," Henry said. "But you're a fairy queen and I'm Prince Charming, so who do you think is going to win?"

She relaxed against him. "You really are my Prince Charming," she sighed.

"And you are my fairy queen," he replied, kissing the top of her head.

"So, what does that make me?" Clarissa asked, entering the room with a pink sweater in her arms.

Henry reached over and pulled her into their hug. "Um, the frog princess?" he teased.

"Daddy!"

"A dwarf?" Becca asked.

4

"Mommy!"

"Well, let me think," Henry said, rubbing his hand over his chin. "How about a fairy princess?"

"A double special fairy princess," she replied.

"Double special?" her mother asked.

"Yes, 'cause I'm a fairy princess and I'm 'dopted," she said.

Henry pulled her closer and kissed the top of her head. "Yes, you were the treasure we found to make our family whole."

"So I'm a fairy princess treasure?" she asked.

"Exactly," her mother said, "our priceless treasure."

# # # #

A few hours later Clarissa lay under the covers in her bed trying to keep her eyes open for just a few more minutes.

"Just one more story, please Daddy?" she asked.

Henry, seated on the side of the bed, leaned forward and rustled her hair with his hand. "You will keep me here begging for one more story until it's morning time," he teased.

She shook her head. "No, I promise," she replied sincerely, a big yawn escaping from her lips. "Just tell me the one about the angels. Then I'll go to sleep."

"Okay, just that one and then you will close your eyes and sleep, right?"

"Uh-huh."

5

"When God created the world he had a plan," he began.

"That all of us would come down here and be born, right?" she interrupted.

Grinning, he nodded. "Right. We would all take our turns and be born and grow up and work really hard to be good."

"Yep, and the jobs of the mommies and the daddies were to take care of the children so they would learn how to be good, right?"

"Exactly right," he said. "But God knew that sometimes people would need extra help."

"So he made angels," she said, her voice soft with awe.

Henry nodded. "Yes," he replied, lowering his voice. "There are angels all around us, just waiting for the right time to help us. They are closer than you think, and they often disguise themselves like regular people."

"So how can you tell if they are angels?" she asked.

"They want you to do good things, like God and Mommy and Daddy would want you to do," he said. "Angels would never have you do something bad."

Clarissa yawned and rubbed her eyes. "Will I ever meet an angel, Daddy?" she asked, as she snuggled into her pillow.

He leaned over and kissed her on her forehead. "I'm sure you will, sweetheart," he said. "You just have to watch for them."

She nodded sleepily. "Night Daddy, I love you."

"I love you too," he whispered, to the already sleeping child.

A fierce feeling of protectiveness struck him as he watched her sleep from the doorway. *There is no way anyone is going to take her from us*, he vowed silently. *Not while I'm alive.*

\# \# \# \#

Henry hated to take a day off work; they really needed every dollar he earned. But Dr. Gary Copper was not only an annoyance; he was also affecting Becca's health and so he needed to be stopped. The look of relief on her face that morning when he explained what he was going to do was enough to reassure him that he'd made the right decision.

The drive to Sycamore took a little over an hour and, if he had been in the right frame of mind, he might have enjoyed the trip down the country lanes surrounded by fields of corn and soybeans. Instead, he rehearsed what he was going to say to Dr. Copper over and over again.

When he finally arrived at the lovely home in the middle of the subdivision, he realized Becca was right. Dr. Copper had money. He had enough money to fight for Clarissa and he had enough money to get the best lawyers and perhaps win.

His stomach began to clench as he walked up the sidewalk to the home and he tried to calm himself down. *I may not have money, but I know Clarissa is where she is supposed to be. She is my daughter, not his. She loves me, not him. She needs me and she needs Becca and no amount of money can replace the love we give to her.*

He thought about Becca's comment the night before, Clarissa growing up too quickly because of Becca's illness. He mentally shook his head. *No. That's what families do. They sacrifice for each other, they learn from serving each other and their love grows. We're giving Clarissa all she needs; love, encouragement and stability.*

With firmer resolve, he confidently strode up the last few steps to the door and pressed the doorbell. A few moments later the door opened and revealed a kindly looking middle-aged man.

Well, this shouldn't be too hard, Henry thought.

"May I help you?" Dr. Copper asked.

"Hello, I'm Henry Madison," he said, noting the look of surprise on Dr. Copper's face. "I'd like to speak with you about my daughter, Clarissa."

Dr. Copper's face broke into a wide welcoming smile. "Well, of course, of course," he said, opening the door wider and stepping aside. "Please come in. Let's have a chat over some light refreshments."

Henry stepped forward into the house. "Well, I don't want to put you out."

"Oh, no, it's not a problem," he replied. "I have an iced tea that's to die for."

Chapter One

"Ohhh, cake," eight-year-old Maggie sighed happily to Mary O'Reilly as Police Chief Bradley Alden approached the table juggling three plates of wedding cake, forks and napkins. He placed the largest piece of cake in front of Maggie and earned an adoring smile from her. "I never get the biggest 'cause I'm the littlest," she confided in them, just before she inserted a large forkful of cake into her mouth and smiled in delight, frosting coating her lips. "Mmmmmmm."

Bradley sat down next to Mary and placed her piece in front of her. Then he followed Maggie's example, helping himself to a generous piece. "This is really good cake," he said, and leaning over to Mary whispered, "This is the second best reason for having a wedding."

"What's the first one?" Maggie asked.

Bradley turned a little red, nonplussed for a moment.

"Why, the lovely dress, of course," Mary said, laughing at Bradley. "What do you think is the best part, Maggie?"

"The kiss," Maggie said, "when they say 'and now you may kiss the bride.' That's the best part."

Maggie turned back to Bradley. "What do you think is the best part?"

"I agree with you," he said. "The kiss is the best part."

"The kiss is the best part of what?" Katie, Maggie's mother, asked as she joined them at the table.

"A wedding," Maggie explained. "Bradley told Mary the wedding cake was the second best part of getting married."

Katie looked over at Bradley and raised one eyebrow in a way mothers have done for generations.

"I whispered it," Bradley stammered, "I promise."

"The whispered stuff is always the best words to listen to," Maggie explained. "My mom and dad whisper all the time, especially when they talk about you-know-what."

"What's you-know-what?" Bradley asked, grinning at Katie.

"I think this conversation should end here and now, young lady," Katie stated, turning a delightful shade of pink.

Maggie shrugged. "I don't know, they always just say you-know-what," she said, before she filled her mouth with her last piece of cake.

Mary snorted and then took a bite of cake before Katie could glare at her.

"Well, I think, perhaps, Maggie and I should be getting home," Katie said.

"So you and Dad can do you-know-what?" Maggie asked.

Nearly spitting out her cake, Mary clasped her hands over her mouth and Bradley hid his laughter in a cough.

Katie turned even redder, shook her head and laughed. "I suppose once you become a parent, you lose all chances for dignity."

"You are the most dignified mom I've ever met," Mary said sincerely. "And you have happy, confident and intelligent children. You are amazing in my book."

"Thank you," Katie replied, helping Maggie from the chair and wiping her mouth with a napkin. "That means a lot to me."

"Katie, I was wondering if Bradley and I could come by this evening?" she asked, turning to Bradley for a quick approval. "We need to talk to you and Clifford about a couple of things."

"Sure, that would be fine," she said. "The kids are generally in their rooms by eight o'clock, so any time after that will give us a chance to visit without interruption."

"Great. We'll be over then," Mary replied.

Bradley waited until Katie and Maggie were out of earshot, moved his chair closer to Mary's and placed his hand over hers. "So, what happened and why do we need to speak with Katie and Clifford?"

Mary turned her hand over, so their fingers could link, and looked into his eyes. "Maggie isn't your daughter," she said softly.

"What? Are you sure?"

The soft words hit him like bricks. Although he hadn't admitted it to himself, he had begun to think of Maggie as his daughter. He had opened his heart to her and now she was being pulled away from him, just like Jeannine.

"But…but she saw Jeannine," he argued. "She spoke with her…"

Mary nodded. "Maggie told me that Jeannine came to her only when her friend, Clarissa spent the night," she explained, "because she could see Jeannine, but Clarissa couldn't and Jeannine wanted to speak with Clarissa."

"What? Who's Clarissa?"

"Maggie said Clarissa was her best friend because they were the 'doption girls," Mary said, repeating Maggie's phrase. "Both girls had been adopted, so they formed a special bond."

"Both girls?" Bradley asked. "So Clarissa…"

"Clarissa is your daughter," Mary said. "Maggie said Jeannine told her that Clarissa was her little girl."

"Where is she?" he asked, rising to his feet. "We should talk to Katie now and get her address. Why did you want to wait?"

Mary stood and put her hand on his shoulder, stopping him from following after Katie and Maggie. "Maggie told me that Clarissa and her mother left town," she explained.

"Where did they go?" he asked, turning toward her.

"I'm hoping we can find that out from Katie and Clifford this evening," Mary explained. "It sounds like something might have happened to Clarissa's father, but I want to confirm the details with them."

He nodded and sighed, and they both sat back down at the table. "It's funny, in some ways I really wanted Maggie to be my daughter," he said, running his hand through his hair. "She is such a loveable child. But then I realize the reason she turned out that way is because of the love and care Katie and Clifford have given her all her life. I wondered how I could ever tell them she was mine?"

Mary was silent for a moment. "You know…" she finally said.

"What?"

"Tonight, when we meet with them and tell them the truth…they might be a little…I don't know…apprehensive of our relationship with both Maggie and Andy," she said.

"A little suspicious of our motives, being so willing to take care of the kids?"

Nodding, Mary replied, "We didn't…couldn't tell them what we suspected, but they might not see it that way."

He took her hand in his once again. "I'm sorry, Mary," he said. "I know how much you love them. If Katie and Clifford feel threatened and keep the kids away from you, it's because of me. I didn't mean for this to happen."

Mary shrugged. "Of course you didn't. And besides, it wasn't just your decision to keep it from them. We all decided it would be best. Let's not think about the negative side right now. Let's just hope they understand the predicament we were in and why we did what we did."

"What we need is a diplomat who can convince them that our decision was the best for all concerned," Bradley said. "And that we really had no choice."

They both looked at each other and smiled. "Ian."

Chapter Two

Stanley twirled Rosie around one last time as the final chords of the song faded away. She laughed with delight as he bent her over into a not-so-deep dip and gave her a quick kiss.

"Oh, Stanley, you are such a wonderful dancer," Rosie gushed, waving her hand in front of her face to cool herself from the exertion. "Wherever did you learn those moves?"

Smiling, Stanley shrugged his shoulders modestly. "Well, I ain't saying I'm good and I ain't saying I'm not. But I will say it makes all the difference iffen you got a good partner and I can tell you, I was dancing with the best."

"Oh, Stanley," Rosie said, a soft blush stealing across her cheeks, "you say the nicest things."

Stanley put his arm around her shoulders and started to lead her off the dance floor when he saw Mary and Bradley sitting at the table in the far corner of the reception hall.

"Why ain't Mary dancing?" he wondered aloud. "Seems to me that girl needs a little more fun in her life."

"Well, it looks like they might be discussing something serious," Rosie said.

"Those two are always being serious," Stanley scoffed. "'Bout time he did something romantical. Come on Rosie, someone's got to talk some sense into that young man."

He guided Rosie across the room and stopped in front of Mary and Bradley's table.

"So, girlie, why ain't you out there cutting up a rug?" Stanley asked Mary, and then he shot Bradley an annoyed look. "Ain't no one got the manners to ask you?"

Mary placed her hand over her mouth, trying to hide the smile, and shook her head. "We've been talking..." she began.

"You get the chance to hold a pretty girl in your arms and all you want to do is talk to her?" Stanley asked Bradley. "In my day, real men didn't pass on an opportunity like that."

The soft strains of a love song began to play and couples, young and old, began to drift out onto the dance floor. Bradley stood up. "Excuse us, please," Bradley said. "I've got a pretty girl I need to hold in my arms."

He turned to Mary. "Mary, may I have the pleasure of this dance?"

She smiled up at him and nodded. "I would be delighted."

He led her to the dance floor and pulled her into his arms. She laid her cheek against his shoulder as they swayed gently to the slow song. She inhaled his unique masculine scent and, as always, it caused her insides to begin a slow meltdown.

She wondered what it was about his cologne that caused her reaction. She inhaled the scent again and felt the tingle deep inside. She was sure there were pheromones mixed in with the woodsy scent and...something else. She cuddled closer, burying her nose next to his chest and sniffed again. *Was it citrus or...?* She inhaled deeply. *Yes, citrus definitely. Grapefruit? That was it! And... something...* She sniffed once again. *Maybe ginger...* She started to breathe in again...

"Um, Mary, what are you doing?" Bradley asked.

How embarrassing, she thought.

"Sniffing you," she said, biting her lower lip and lifting her head to meet his eyes.

"Sniffing me?"

She nodded.

"I showered, I promise."

She chortled. "I know. You just smell so...good."

"Good?"

She shrugged slightly. "Your scent causes a meltdown reaction in my body, like there are pheromones in your cologne."

"Meltdown, huh?" he asked, inhaling deeply as a self-satisfied, manly grin spread across his face. "So, have you ever had this reaction with any other man?"

Lowering her face slightly, she smiled. "No," she replied, snuggling back into his arms. "You are the only one whose scent makes me slightly crazy."

He bent down and brushed a kiss along the side of her neck that caused her to shiver. "Good, keep it that way," he whispered.

She sighed softly and reached up, pressing her lips against his neck. "I intend to."

He slid his hand up her back slowly and then threaded his fingers into her hair, pulling back slightly, so he had access to her mouth. "Mary," he said, his voice husky, as he searched her face for a moment and then lowered his face toward hers.

"Mary!" Linda called brightly, as she hurried toward them with Bob in tow. "We're going to be leaving in a few minutes and I just couldn't go without talking to you."

Bradley glanced at Mary, a wry smile on his face, and then loosened his hold on her.

Mary looked over. "Linda, you look so beautiful. Obviously being married agrees with you."

"Well, so far," Linda laughed.

Turning to grin at Bob, Mary chuckled. "Well, that's a good sign. You've been married for about an hour and she still loves you."

He put his arm around Linda's waist and pulled her close. "And I intend to keep her in love with me."

Bradley extended his hand to Bob and the two men shook hands. "Congratulations Bob. I know you are both going to be happy," Bradley said.

"Well, thanks to you and Mary for bringing us together," he replied. "And thanks to Mary's fast reaction during the wedding. You saved my life."

"I had some help," she said, thinking of Ernie, the ghost of Linda's father. "Besides, I'm sure that's one of the responsibilities of being a maid of honor, protecting the married couple from any crazed infiltrators."

"Well, if it's not, it should be," Bob said, leaning forward and kissing Mary's cheek. "Thank you for all you've done for us."

"Really, Bob, it was nothing," she said.

"No, Mary, it was everything," he said sincerely.

Throwing her arms around Mary, Linda hugged her tightly. "Thank you, Mary," she whispered. "You gave my true love back to me twice. I can never repay you."

"Just be happy," Mary said.

"Thank you," Linda said, wiping away a tear.

"Come on, sweetheart, we've got a plane to catch," Bob said, wrapping his arm around her shoulders and pulling her close for a quick kiss. "Besides, these two want to dance."

Linda smiled and nodded. "I'll call you when I get back," she called, as Bob led her across the dance floor.

"Perfect," Mary said.

Bradley drew her back into his arms as another slow song began to play. "The always amazing Mary O'Reilly," he said.

She looked up at him. "Shut up and kiss me," she replied.

His eyebrows shot up a little and a slow smile spread across his face. "It will be my pleasure."

Chapter Three

"Well, and how was the wedding?" Ian asked politely, barely looking up from the computer, as Mary and Bradley walked through the door to Mary's home.

"It was lovely," Mary answered.

"Good, good," Ian replied, his interest in the webpage obvious.

"Action packed," Bradley added.

"Action packed?" Ian repeated, not really aware of the words. "Well, isn't that nice."

"Mary ended up going three rounds with Linda's stepfather. Knocked him out cold with a smooth uppercut to his chin. The guy had a glass jaw."

Ian lifted his head from the screen. "Do you mind repeating what you just said?"

Mary grinned at Bradley and then walked past Ian to the kitchen and began to fill the teapot with water.

"Bradley, would you like some tea?" she asked.

Bradley pulled out his smartphone and began tapping on the face. "Don't mind if I do, thank you Mary," he said.

"Oh, no, you kinna be thinking you'll walk in here and drop a bombshell as that was and not explain yourselves away," Ian demanded.

Mary looked over at him. "I'm sorry, did you say something?" she asked sweetly.

"Aye, I'll be begging your pardon for not paying attention the first time," he said. "Now, what's this about you going a few rounds at the wedding? Was it during the reception?"

Mary put the teapot on the stove and hurried over to sit next to him on the couch. "Do you remember Ernie, the ghost that appeared during our bedroom snowball fight?"

Bradley looked up from his phone. "Excuse me? Bedroom snowball fight?"

Mary glanced over at Bradley. "Oh that, it was nothing. Really. I'll tell you about it later."

Ian chortled. "Aye, and I want to be around for the telling."

Bradley stared at Ian. "Oh, you will be, believe me."

Rolling her eyes, Mary turned back to Ian. "So Ernie taught me how to box because he said it was important, something he needed me to do for a loved one. But he said he couldn't tell me the reason."

"Okay, so Ernie taught you how to box," Ian said. "But you didna know why."

"Right," Mary replied. "And then, today, I was standing at the front of the church and the minister was about to start the ceremony, when

Linda's stepfather walked in through a back door and pointed a gun at Bob, the groom."

"So, the stepfather didna want Linda to marry Bob?"

"No, the stepfather didn't want Linda to get married at all, because she was his meal ticket," she replied.

"So, the stepfather is ready to shoot Bob, and Mary drops her bouquet on the ground, punches him in the stomach and follows up with a jab in the side," Bradley said. "He drops his gun and it skids across the floor. Then Mary dances around him like a prizefighter…"

Mary brought her arms up in a fighting stance and shadow boxed for a moment. "Fly like an eagle and punch like a…" She paused, thinking for a moment and then, smiling, added, "Punch like a bee."

Ian and Bradley grinned. "Or something like that," Ian said.

"So Mary basically takes him out in a matter of moments, knocked cold, on the floor," Bradley said. "So fast no one else had time to help her."

"In a dress and heels," Mary added with a wink.

"Well, now, that was truly amazing," Ian said. "And will you be giving up your day job to start a career in the ring?"

"No way! Boxing hurts," she admitted, shaking her hands for emphasis. "Besides, all kidding aside, I couldn't have done it without Linda's father."

"Oh, Linda's father was there too, was he?" Ian asked.

"Yes, he was the one who encouraged me to fight," Mary explained impatiently. "He used to be a boxer."

"Well, then, why didn't he fight the bloke?"

"Because he was a ghost," Mary said with an exasperated sigh.

Ian smiled. "Aye, only in the world of Mary O'Reilly does a dead man attend his daughter's wedding."

Mary shook her head. "No, only in the world of Mary O'Reilly do you know about it," she said. "I'm sure there are many fathers who, although they can't be there in body, are there in spirit."

Nodding, Ian said, "You have the right of it, Mary."

"So, after Ernie kissed Linda…"

"Why did Ernie kiss Linda?"

"Because Ernie is Linda's father," Mary said, rolling her eyes once again. "Pay attention Ian. So, after Ernie kissed Linda, he said goodbye to me and faded away."

"Well, that was quite a fairytale wedding," Ian said, with a smile. "So, tell me, was the rest of the day uneventful?"

There was a moment of silence in the room as Bradley met Mary's eyes and sighed. "Well, I suppose there was another significant event," he admitted. "Mary learned that Maggie is not my daughter."

Ian's face sobered. "Oh, I'm so sorry," he said. "Mary, what did you discover?"

"Maggie and I were at a table and she told me that she missed Mike, and I..." Mary's voice cracked and she took a deep breath, as her eyes filled with tears.

She tried to speak but couldn't at first. Finally she wiped her eyes and whispered. "And I told her I missed him too."

"Aye, we all miss him," Ian said sympathetically.

Mary nodded and continued, her voice a little stronger. "I explained to her that he wanted to say goodbye to her, but everything happened so quickly, he couldn't. Then she told me the same thing had happened with the sad lady, Jeannine. She had asked Maggie to say goodbye to Clarissa for her because she had to leave."

"Who is Clarissa?" Ian asked.

"Well, it seems that Clarissa is my daughter," Bradley replied.

Chapter Four

Clarissa Madison sat on the cold wood floor, her feet tucked inside her flannel nightgown for warmth. She blew on the window and watched a small patch of frost melt away. The blurry neon lights from the bar across the street were now clear and she could watch the comings and goings on the sidewalk. She scooted up on her knees, her elbows resting on the scarred wooden windowsill, and looked intently down at the patrons. *Would she be able to tell from this far away?* she wondered.

A man and woman walked from the alley toward the front door. The man had his arm around the woman's shoulders and he was whispering into her ear. She laughed loudly and threw her head back and Clarissa studied her face. Bright red rouge defined her sharp cheekbones and dark cobalt eye shadow accentuated the thick black liner coating the lids of her eyes. Her lips glowed with crimson and her big teeth gleamed with a yellow hue.

Clarissa shook her head. *No, she couldn't be one. She just couldn't.*

Standing, she hurried across the room to the little desk in the corner and pulled the oversized library book from her backpack. It was too dark in her room to read the title. She knew she couldn't turn on her light, because she didn't want to disturb her mother, who slept on the small couch in the living room, just outside of her room.

She walked back to the window and angled the book, so the flashing neon sign threw beams of red, orange and green across its cover. *A Book of Angels.* Clarissa compared the title to the bar sign across the street. "Angel's Bar" flickered in all the colors of a neon rainbow. Next to the name was a fluorescent image of a scantily clad woman with wings that, through the magic of animated neon lighting, lifted up to expose more of her bikini clad body and then dropped down to present a more modest image.

She knew her daddy was an angel now, but she didn't think he looked anything like the girl on the sign. She was sure her daddy would always look like he did when he came home from work every day, smelling of wood and the peppermint gum he always had in his car. She paused for a moment; *did angels get to wear work boots?* If so, she knew he would be in those scarred brown leather boots.

She still couldn't believe he was dead. They had a funeral; she saw his body lying in the coffin. But he didn't really look like her daddy. It was like her real daddy got pulled out of his body and just left the shell, like the caterpillar's cocoon in Mrs. Leverton's class two years ago. The cocoon was empty and there was a beautiful butterfly in the cage.

She sighed softly. Instead of butterfly wings, her mommy told her that Daddy had angel wings now. She closed her eyes and pictured her big, tall daddy with white wings and giggled softly. He might look pretty silly, but he would look better than any of the people coming in or out of the building she was watching.

Clarissa smiled and hugged the book to her chest. "There's angels 'cross the street, Daddy," she whispered. "Just like you used to say. Angels to watch over Mommy and me."

She looked down on the bar and shook her head. "'Cept I can't tell which ones are the angels," she admitted softly.

She blew on the window again and the patch of clear glass appeared again. Propping her head against the thin glass pane, she studied each patron, hoping to find a celestial being among them. When she heard the coughing begin in the next room, she tightened her arms around the book and closed her eyes.

"Please God and Daddy, if you're listening," she whispered, "help Mommy feel better. Please help us go back to Freeport. Please make the bad man go away. Please make us not so scared. Amen."

But the coughing continued. She heard her mother cross the living room and slowly walk down the hall to the bathroom. When the bathroom door closed, Clarissa jumped up and hurried to the bedroom door. She opened it a crack and listened. When the muted coughing was interrupted by heaving and vomiting, Clarissa's stomach tightened. She remembered when she had the flu and she threw up in the toilet. She remembered it hurt her throat, but after it happened she felt a little better. But her mother threw up every night and she didn't think it made her feel better at all.

She heard the toilet flush and the water run in the sink. In a moment her mother would be returning to bed. She knew she should close her door and get back in bed, but she wanted to see her mother, to make sure she was fine. She pushed the door, so it was nearly closed and watched her mother slowly walk back up the hall, her hand against the wall for support. Pausing to take a shaky breath, her mother looked as if she was going to collapse before her. Clarissa knew she needed to help her.

Slowly opening her door, Clarissa stepped out, yawned widely and rubbed her hands over her eyes.

"Clarissa," her mother said weakly. "Why aren't you asleep?"

Clarissa stumbled forward, in a mock half-asleep manner. "Oh, I woke up and I was thirsty," she lied, wrapping her arms around her mother's waist. "Were you thirsty too?"

Her mother nodded. "Yes, yes, I was," she said, her voice weak and tired. "Why don't you go back to bed and I'll get us both water."

Tightening her arms around her mother, she shook her head. "No, it's my turn to get water," she insisted, as she guided her mother back to the couch. "You lie down and let me get it. I'm real good at getting water."

Her mother crumpled onto the couch and Clarissa tucked the covers around her. "Is there anything else you want from the kitchen, Mommy?" she asked. "Do you want some of your medicine?"

Her mother shook her head. "No, Clarissa, I'm all out of my medicine," she said. "I'll get some more tomorrow. Just water will be fine."

Clarissa bent over her mother and gave her a kiss on her cheek. "Okay, Mommy. You just rest and I'll get us water. And don't worry; Daddy's going to send us angels."

A single tear formed in her mother's eye and slid slowly down her cheek. She lifted her hand and gently stroked Clarissa's cheek. "That will be wonderful, darling. Angels are just what we need."

Chapter Five

Mary, Bradley and Ian climbed up the stairs of the Brennan's front porch. They paused before knocking on the door.

"We have to be honest," Mary said, "totally honest."

"Even if it makes us look like a bunch of daft loons running about after things we can't see?" Ian asked.

"Well, we can see them," she countered. "They can't see them. Besides, it's not like it's totally unbelievable. Bradley believed."

Clearing his throat and glancing away from his friends for a moment, he paused before answering. "Even after witnessing Earl thumping through your house in the middle of the night, I still had my doubts," he said. "It wasn't until I was able to see them when I touched you, that I really began to believe."

She exhaled slowly. "Well, I don't think we're going to get any supernatural help," she said. "But, even if they think we're nuts, we have to tell them the truth."

Ian nodded. "Aye, if for nothing else, it will help prepare the way for Maggie if she ever decides to let them know about her gift," he agreed.

Bradley leaned forward and knocked on the door. Mary, standing between the two men, grabbed hold of their hands and squeezed. "For luck," she whispered.

"For luck then," Ian agreed.

"Can't hurt," Bradley added.

The door opened and Katie stood before them, a wide smile on her face. "We thought you would never knock," she said with a laugh. "Please come in out of the cold."

"We were just having a wee chat before we came in," Ian explained.

Clifford walked up behind her. "Well, it would be much warmer to chat inside," he said, standing back and letting them enter the house.

Stepping into the Brennan home was a step back in time for Mary. Organized clutter is what her mother used to call it. The home of a busy family; with hooks for coats and backpacks next to the door, rubber mats for boots and shoes underneath the coats and a bookshelf of cubbyholes for papers, art projects and anything else that could fit. The couches and chairs were overstuffed and well-used, the perfect place to sit when reading a book to a child or several children. There were precious objects d'art Brennan-style scattered across walls and other surfaces. But most of all, Mary could feel the love and peace inside the walls of the house and desperately hoped their conversation with the Brennans would not do anything to alter it.

"I love your house," Mary said, glancing around. "It reminds me of my house when I was growing up."

Katie smiled. "Well, it's nice to hear that you lived in a home like this and grew up to be a fairly normal person."

"Fairly normal," Ian teased.

"Which brings us to the purpose of our meeting with you," Bradley said.

"The fact that Mary is only fairly normal?" Clifford asked with a laugh.

"Actually, yes," Bradley replied, in a more serious vein.

Both Katie and Clifford paused for a moment, their smiles dropping slightly. "Well, let me take your coats and hang them up," Katie said. "And you can follow Clifford to the kitchen table. Help yourselves to tea and cookies."

They followed Clifford to the country-style kitchen and each took a place around the large oak table. Ian leaned over and picked up the teapot. "Shall I pour?" he asked.

"Please," Clifford replied.

Ian poured tea and passed the cups around while they waited for Katie to come into the room.

A few moments later she entered the room and took her place at the table. "I just checked on the kids," she said. "They're all asleep, so we shouldn't be disturbed. And I have to admit, you have me just a little bit worried."

"Oh, there's nothing to worry about," Mary assured her. "We just need to talk to you about some things…"

She faltered.

"Aye, fill you in about some things we've learned in the past couple of months," Ian added. "That might be able to help you…"

"And, in turn, you might be able to help us," Bradley finished.

"You really haven't eased my mind," Katie said as she slipped into a chair at the table and picked up a teacup.

Ian picked up the teapot and filled her cup. "Really, it's not so hard as all that," he said. "Although, you might need to keep an open mind to some of the things we're going to talk about."

Katie nodded. "Okay, I'm ready."

Mary turned to Katie and Clifford, took a deep breath and began. "I don't know if you knew that I was a police officer in Chicago before I moved here," Mary said.

"I think I remember hearing that," Clifford said. "Maybe Andy mentioned it."

Mary smiled. "He does tend to have very good hearing. Yes, I was a police officer and I was…" she paused, hesitant to continue.

Bradley reached across the table, placed his hand over hers and gave her a nod of encouragement.

"I was shot," she finished, sending Bradley a grateful smile. "I was rushed to the hospital. Emergency surgery. And I died."

"What?" Clifford asked. "I don't understand."

"I remember walking toward a bright light and thinking, 'Okay, wow, there is a light. I guess I'm dead,'" she said, a little flippantly.

Then her voice softened as she continued, "But then someone called my name and I stopped moving toward the light. This voice…it was like it was both inside of me and outside of me, but I could hear it clearly."

The memory of the encounter played in her mind for a moment and she paused as she remembered. Shaking her head slightly, she continued, "Anyway, the voice said I had a choice. I could continue to the light and wait for my family to join me someday or I could go back, but things would be different."

"Obviously you choose to come back," Katie said.

Mary nodded. "Yes, I didn't want to leave my family," she explained. "I didn't want my brother…anyone…to feel guilty about my death."

"So, what was different?" Clifford asked.

Taking a deep breath, Mary met their eyes. "When I came back, I discovered that I could see and communicate with ghosts."

"Ghosts?" Clifford asked, shaking his head. "Are you kidding?"

Ian saw both surprise and doubt in Clifford's face. "It's not uncommon for people who have had a near-death experience to come back with extrasensory gifts," he explained. "I've not only done studies about it in the UK, I've also experienced it myself."

"Wait! You're telling me you can see ghosts too?" Clifford said. "Is this some joke or are you all just plain crazy?"

He stood up, his chair scraping against the floor. "We let you watch our children," he said, his eyes widening with sudden fear. "You didn't tell them...you didn't expose them to your fantasies?"

"Of course not," Mary cried.

"Mary would have never..." Bradley began.

"They wouldn't have to," Katie answered calmly. "Our Maggie can see ghosts all on her own."

Everyone stopped and stared at Katie.

"You knew?" Mary asked.

"What the hell?" Clifford asked.

"I'm sorry, Cliff," Katie said. "I've known that Maggie could see things since she was little. When she was a baby, I'd catch her lying in her crib, looking around the room and laughing at things I couldn't see. At first I just thought she was seeing angels, but as she got older and started having conversations, I suspected it might be spirits or ghosts."

Clifford turned to Katie. "Why didn't you tell me?" he asked.

"Well, I didn't think it was something you'd really want to know," she replied.

Sighing, he sat back down in his chair. "My grandmother used to tell me she could see ghosts and

I always thought she was nuts," he confessed. "I always told her there were no such things as ghosts."

Bradley laughed softly. "Yeah, well, that's what I thought a couple of months ago, until I met Mary and my whole perspective changed."

Clifford turned to Bradley. "What changed your mind?"

"Seeing a ghost for myself."

"You actually saw one?"

Bradley nodded. "Yeah, and I thought I was going nuts."

Clifford turned to Mary. "Is this for real? Is there a purpose to it, or is it just a cool parlor trick?"

"It's real," Mary said, "and it's not a trick, I promise."

"She's solved a number of local murder cases," Ian said. "Ghosts don't just appear to her, they seek her out when they have unfinished business that's keeping them here."

"Mary was able to solve the murder of my wife using her talents," Bradley added. "If not for her, I still wouldn't know what happened to Jeannine or to my daughter."

"You have a daughter?" Katie asked.

Bradley ran his hand through his hair and sighed. "Yes, I do," he said. "And that's the main reason we're here tonight."

Chapter Six

The television glowed in the darkened living room and emitted the voices of an evening news show host who held conservative political leanings and the noted celebrity he was interviewing. Stanley Wagner snorted as he lifted up the remote and pressed the mute button. "Who cares what that nincompoop thinks?" he grumbled, standing and making his way from the living room into the kitchen. "Why the hell does he think that just because he can act in a movie, I'm supposed to consider him an expert on politics?"

He switched on the under-cabinet light and pulled a saucepan out of the drawer. Placing it on his butcher-block counter, he turned to take the milk out of the refrigerator across the room. On his way, he spotted the remainders of the strawberry rhubarb pie Rosie had brought him. A lopsided grin spread across his face. *Yeah, asking Rosie to marry me is one of the best decisions I ever made*, he thought.

Pulling the milk carton out and grabbing the pie plate, he placed them both on the counter next to the oven. He poured a generous cupful of milk into the pan and set it on a low flame on the stove. Reaching up to the cabinet above his head, he pulled down a small plate and immediately filled it with an oversized piece of pie.

"Nothing like a little snack before bed," he said, wiping the knife with his finger and licking the filling off. "Yes, sirree, tart and sweet, just the way I like my women too."

He reached over to the silverware drawer to pull out a fork when he caught a movement out of the corner of his eye. Something, no someone, had just moved across the hallway between his bedroom and the bathroom. Dropping the fork back into the drawer, he walked across the kitchen to the hall. He flipped on the lights and looked around. The bathroom was empty and so was the bedroom. He moved into the bedroom and checked the windows and the closet.

"I ain't going crazy," he muttered. "I seen something."

Kneeling down on the floor, he checked under his bed and, except for a few dust bunnies, found it empty too. Grabbing the side of the bed to help get back up; he realized his next mistake as soon as he heard the unmistakable sizzle. He rushed out of the room back to the kitchen in time to watch the hot milk overflow onto the stovetop. Grabbing a hot pad, he picked up the pan and carried to the sink, letting it cool down while he cleaned up the mess on the stove. He picked up a roll of paper towels and started mopping up the milk when he froze and turned back to the hall.

The light had been off. The hallway had been dark. Whatever he saw had its own light source.

Whatever he saw had been glowing. A chill ran down his spine and he shook it off.

"I'm a grown man," he said loudly. "Ain't gonna get spooked in my own home. You hear me. I ain't going to get spooked."

The light in the hallway turned off by itself.

Stanley took a deep breath. "Well, maybe I ain't and maybe I am," he whispered.

####

Rosie Pettigrew leaned forward over the bathroom sink and peered into the mirror, staring intently at her reflection. Without shifting her eyes, she reached down, picked up a plastic tube and squeezed a small amount of white cream onto her finger. She dabbed the ointment lightly into the fragile skin beneath her eyes and then patted the area until it disappeared into her skin. Glancing a little lower into the mirror, she studied what her gaping nightgown neckline revealed, looked down at the tube in her hand and shook her head. "There isn't a tube large enough to lift and firm those," she said with a giggle. "Oh well, Stanley didn't fall in love with a twenty-year-old, so he'd better not be expecting one."

She put the lid back on the tube, placed it in her cosmetic drawer, flipped off the bathroom light and walked into her bedroom. Smiling, she took a moment to look around the room. Bathed in soft light from the lamp on the nightstand, the soft pink hue of the floral bedspread matched perfectly with the blush-colored carpeting and curtains. Bright accent pillows of sage green, plum and periwinkle on the bed and a pale pink chaise lounge picked up the delicate flowers from the spread and made the decor more vibrant. A tall rose-colored vase stood in the corner of the room holding a bouquet of silk tiger lilies that added a delicate sophistication.

Walking over to the small vanity, she stroked the antique sterling silver brush and mirror that lay on the marble top and sighed with satisfaction. This room was everything the closet-sized bedroom she had as a child had not been. She had meticulously picked out every detail, even painting the walls herself. This was more than a bedroom, this was a statement. Rosie Pettigrew had made it. She had pulled herself up by her bootstraps and gotten out of the muck and quicksand of her childhood. She had left the feelings of worthlessness and inadequacy behind and replaced them with self-assurance and love. She glanced in the mirror and smiled. She liked herself, saggy parts and all. And that was the most important gift she'd ever given to herself. She had discarded all the unkind labels her father and those like him had placed on her. She wasn't ugly. She wasn't stupid. She wasn't unlovable. She was a wonderful person, a good friend, and worthy of love and care.

"Welcome to the Rosie Pettigrew fan club," she said, turning to the top of her dresser where a number of small picture frames stood. "Our numbers may be small, but they are growing every day."

She was drawn to the newest one where she was in the middle of a photo with Maggie and Andy Brennan. The two children were smiling widely, their lips covered in chocolate frosting from licking the beaters. She remembered Mary insisting on taking the picture and the two children waiting until the last moment and then turning and placing chocolate kisses on either side of her face. She could almost smell the Dutch chocolate from the frosting. And she could remember the warmth from their innocent display of love.

Glancing at the other photos, she smiled at the collection of her friends; Mary, Bradley, Ian and, finally, Stanley. She took a deep breath. Stanley.

She picked up the silver frame and studied the face looking back at her. He hadn't wanted to have his photo taken and he had declared he wasn't going to smile. She cajoled, pleaded and bribed, but nothing seem to work until, finally, she simply said, "Stanley, this is important to me," and he immediately lifted his wrinkled cheeks into the closest semblance of a smile she'd ever seen coming from him. She almost expected his face to crack from the use of those muscles that hadn't been exercised in years.

Chuckling, she lifted the photo to her face, she gently kissed his picture. "Good night, sweetheart," she said. "Sweet dreams."

Gently laying the frame back on her dresser, she crossed the room and climbed into her bed. She leaned across and turned off the lamp on the nightstand, grabbed the gel-filled night mask and situated it over her eyes. Then, with a smile on her lips, she scooted beneath the covers and snuggled into her pillow.

As soon as her head hit the pillow, her closet door soundlessly opened. Slowly, first one inch, then two and soon, the door was wide open. From the depths of the closet, a dark figure floated into the room. It was as tall as a man and was hulking in size. It hovered several inches above the floor and wavered next to the closet for only a moment. In the blink of an eye, the figure swept across the room, stopping at the edge of Rosie's bed. Slowing, it hovered next to the bed, moving around the edges, studying the resting woman.

Rosie, blinded by her mask, lifted her pillow, plumped it several times, placed it back down on the bed and snuggled back into it. The figure merely observed her, waiting patiently. Within moments, her soft rhythmic breathing confirmed she was asleep.

Rising into the air, the figure hovered inches above the sleeping woman and finally dropped down to lie beside her. Rosie moved in her sleep, inching away, but the specter followed. She shook her head. "No, leave me alone," she moaned in her sleep.

A brittle mocking laugh echoed in the quiet room.

Rosie sat up in bed, ripping the mask off her face. Frantically she reached for her bedside lamp and, with shaking hands, turned it on. Light flooded into the room and she scanned the area wildly. Taking deep calming breaths, she realized nothing was out of place. Her room looked the same way it had just minutes ago when she had gone to sleep.

"I must have been dreaming," she said aloud, shaking her head. "I just scared myself."

She began to reach for her mask when she saw the closet door was open.

"I thought I..." her last words caught in her throat as she looked down. Her mask lay in the middle of an imprint of a body made by someone else lying in her bed.

Chapter Seven

"Your wife was murdered and your baby daughter was given up for adoption?" Katie asked, her eyes wide with horror after Bradley explained the circumstances behind Jeannine's death. "How did you ever go on with your life?"

Bradley sat back in his chair. "Well, it wasn't until recently that I learned what actually happened to Jeannine and my daughter," he explained. "Mary was able to help Jeannine's ghost remember what happened and we were able to finally catch the man who kidnapped her."

Mary nodded. "We just discovered that his daughter was given up for adoption to a couple in Freeport," Mary said. "But the records are still sealed, so we haven't been able to discover anything else about her."

Katie chuckled. "You must have thought it ironic when I told you Maggie was adopted."

Mary and Bradley glanced at each other, neither saying a word. Finally, Ian replied with a nervous laugh of his own. "Oh, aye, it was quite ironic."

"Wait…" Clifford said, eying the three of them. "You thought Maggie was Bradley's daughter, didn't you?"

Clearing his throat, Bradley nodded. "Yes, Clifford, for a little while we thought she might be my daughter."

"But...but...why didn't you come to us? Ask us?" Katie asked.

"Actually, that was our first impulse," Mary explained. "It seemed so logical. Not only was she adopted, but Maggie admitted to us that she'd seen a ghost, a sad lady named Jeannine."

Katie covered her hand with her mouth. "Jeannine...Bradley's wife?" Katie finally asked. "Maggie had seen her?"

Nodding, Mary turned to Katie. "Yes, she had. And we thought, eight years old, a little girl, adopted, in Freeport and she talked about a sad lady, a ghost, coming to see her. What were the odds?"

"And you considered talking to us?" Clifford repeated.

"Aye, we did," Ian interrupted. "But because we were still working with the judge in Chicago to open the files, we didn't think it would be fair to suggest it without proof. We didn't want all of us living in this limbo together."

"And, quite frankly, we didn't want to hurt any of you," Bradley added. "The very reason Maggie is so adorable and bright is because of the way you raised her. You are her parents, no matter what the file might have shown. Your boys are her brothers."

He paused and ran his hand through his hair. "I was actually relieved when we found out that she wasn't the one."

"Wait, what? When did you find that out?" Clifford asked.

"Actually, this afternoon at the wedding," Mary replied. "Maggie explained to me that Jeannine, Bradley's wife, only visited her in order to have her relay messages to her friend, Clarissa."

Nodding, Katie sat back in her chair. "Of course, the 'doption girls," she said. "They were always together, and I do recall Maggie telling Clarissa something the sad lady said. I had no idea that she was her birth mother."

"Now listen," Clifford said. "Becca, Clarissa's mother, has been through enough these past few years. She doesn't need you rushing in and trying to take her daughter from her. She's already had someone try and do that."

"What?" Bradley asked, nearly jumping out of his chair.

Katie shrugged. "There was a man who called them insisting he was the birth father and he wanted Clarissa back. It happened just before Henry, Becca's husband, died."

"Do you happen to know the name of the man who was trying to get Clarissa?" Ian asked.

Katie shrugged. "No one really, he was a dentist..."

"Do you really think this is relevant?" Clifford asked. "Don't you think...?"

"Aye, the man who kidnapped and raped Bradley's wife was a dentist," Ian interrupted. "And as we were working to solve Jeannine's murder, he kidnapped Mary and tried to do the same to her. Don't you think Becca would be better off having someone to lean on, someone to help her?"

Clifford stood up, paced away from the table and then turned back. "Are you telling me there really was a threat to that family? We all thought…"

"Thought what?" Bradley asked.

Clifford sighed. "We thought Becca had made it all up. That she didn't want to acknowledge her husband died in a car accident, falling asleep at the wheel of his car…"

"Wait, what did Becca say?" Mary asked.

"She said that Henry, her husband, had taken the morning off to drive to Sycamore and meet with the dentist who had been calling them, demanding the custody of Clarissa," Clifford said. "Henry knew that it was causing Becca a great deal of stress and…"

"And she had been very sick for a long time," Katie finished. "One of the things the dentist had said was he felt he could take care of Clarissa better than they could. Becca was sure he knew about her illness."

"So did Henry go to Sycamore?" Mary asked.

Katie nodded. "Yes, and on the way home he must have fallen asleep at the wheel," she explained. "He drove into the median and hit a cement pylon head-on. They said he was killed instantly."

"Did they check his system for drugs?" Bradley asked.

"Hey, Henry was a good guy," Clifford asserted. "He didn't use drugs."

"No, no, not that way," Mary explained. "Gary Copper, the dentist, was known for drugging people. He would often lace their drinks with drugs that would knock them out. He could have drugged Henry."

Katie clapped her hand over her mouth. "So she wasn't imagining it," she said. "He really could have been murdered."

"More than likely," Ian said. "Did they do an autopsy?"

Clifford shook his head. "We don't know," he said. "Becca disappeared with Clarissa the next day. Emptied out her checking account and drove away, leaving her house and belongings. She was sure that dentist, Gary Copper, was coming for them."

"When did all of this happen?" Mary asked.

"Almost a year ago," Katie replied, "late last spring."

"Do you have any idea where they might have gone?" Bradley asked. "Did she give you any clue?"

"She said she was going back home, so she could get lost in the crowds," Katie said. "She was from Chicago."

"Did she have any family there?" Bradley asked.

"No, they just had each other," Katie replied, shaking her head. "I remember her saying that. They just had each other."

Chapter Eight

Clarissa awoke to the sun shining through her bedroom window. She slowly stretched her arms up over her head, then pushed the blankets down and hopped out of bed. The wood floor was cold on her bare feet as she crossed the room and opened her door.

The living room was also bathed in sunlight. Sun shone through the windows onto her mother who was still sleeping on the old couch. Clarissa tiptoed over and sighed with silent relief to hear the gentle breathing of a normal sleep. She glanced at the clock on the table next to the couch. It was seven-thirty. Her mother must be working the late shift today or she would already be up and getting dressed.

She padded down the hall to the kitchen and opened the refrigerator door. Other than a small jar of grape jelly, another jar of peanut butter and some small packets of condiments from fast food places, white Styrofoam boxes lined the shelves.

"Let's see what Mommy brought home last night," Clarissa whispered.

She opened a box that held the remainder of the special of the day, spaghetti and meatballs. Another box contained macaroni and cheese, and still another contained fat congealed pot roast and vegetables.

"Gross," she said, wrinkling her nose. "Didn't you bring home anything for breakfast?"

The last container held some rolls, a pile of bacon and two slices of cherry pie. "Yes," she whispered, "pie for breakfast!"

Climbing up on a chair, she retrieved two plastic plates from the cabinet. She put the bacon on one plate and put it into the old microwave on the counter. Pressing the "HIGH" button for ten seconds, she let the microwave work while she made a breakfast plate for her mother. Breaking open a roll, she emptied a container of mayonnaise and ketchup onto it. Once the bacon was reheated, she broke it into roll sized pieces and placed them on the roll. "BLT's just the way Mom likes them," she said.

She slid the bigger piece of pie onto her mother's plate and, with a fork and napkin in hand, carried breakfast into her mother.

Becca lay on the couch, her eyes open, her body aching, trying to get the strength to get out of bed. She had run out of theophylline, her medicine, two days earlier and she felt as if her lungs were closing up on her. If she was going to keep working she had to get more medicine. She slowly inhaled, trying to fill her damaged lungs as full as possible, and then exhaled, wincing at the pain. She started to inhale again when she heard Clarissa coming down the hallway. She took a quick gasp of air, pasted a smile on her face and turned toward her daughter.

"Oh, my, what has Chef Clarissa prepared for us this morning?" she asked brightly, though her words came out in a weak wheeze.

Clarissa smiled, pretending she didn't notice the weakness. "I made you BLT's just the way you like them," she said, putting the plate on the table next to the couch. "And there's delicious cherry pie for dessert. But you have to eat your breakfast first."

"Since when do we have dessert with breakfast?" Becca asked.

"Since today," Clarissa answered. "Because it's a sunny day and it's Sunday. Do you have to go to work today, Mommy?"

Becca nodded. "Yes, but not until this afternoon," she said, reaching for the sandwich and taking a small bite. "This is just delicious, sweetheart."

"It's 'cause I'm a chef," Clarissa said, then her smile left her face and she sighed. "Do I have to go to Mrs. Gunderson's house today?"

Becca lifted her hand and stroked Clarissa's cheek. "Yes, sweetheart, I'm afraid you do," she replied. "But what if we go to the nursing home and talk to the grandmas and grandpas this morning first?"

"But the last time we went there, you got sick," Clarissa said.

Becca closed her eyes for a moment; she hated to see that worried look in her little girl's eyes. She opened her eyes and turned back to Clarissa. "I wasn't sick," she said. "I was just a little dizzy.

Sometimes the smells at the nursing home make me feel that way. It will probably happen again, but don't worry. You just keep singing to them and I'll find a bathroom and be back with you in a few minutes."

"Really?" Clarissa asked.

"Really," Becca replied. "Now, get your breakfast so we can get over to the nursing home before it's too late."

# # # #

Forty minutes later they had walked the four blocks to the inner city nursing home and were signing their names at the reception desk.

"Good morning, Clarissa," Goldie, the receptionist, greeted them with a friendly smile. "Are you going to sing to us again today?"

Clarissa nodded. "Is that okay if I sing to the grandmas and grandpas?" she asked. "Are they awake today?"

Goldie laughed. "Well, some of them is and some of them ain't," she said. "But they all love a good show and they doubly love cute little girls."

Clarissa liked the sound her shoes made against the hard linoleum floor, *click, click, clack.* She stomped her feet harder to make the noise louder.

"Shhh, Clarissa," Becca said. "There are some people who are still asleep here."

Instantly remorseful, Clarissa began to tiptoe. "Sorry, Mom, I forgot."

Becca smiled down at her daughter. "I like the sounds your shoes make too," she whispered.

"Maybe we can go to a museum some day and then your shoes can echo even louder."

"Really?" Clarissa asked, excitement sparkling in her eyes. "When?"

Becca's smile lessened for a moment. "Well, soon, I hope," she replied, reaching over and patting her daughter on her head. "Very soon."

"Can angels hear shoes?"

Her mother stopped walking and looked down at her. "Why, I imagine they could," she said. "Especially loud ones like yours."

Clarissa giggled. "Then we should go to a museum soon," she announced. "So Daddy can hear my shoes."

Sudden tears formed in Becca's eyes and she quickly wiped them away. "Yes. Yes we should," she replied, "because Daddy always liked your loud noises."

Nodding, Clarissa glanced down at her shoes. "And he never got to see these shoes, did he? 'Cause we got these at our special store."

Becca nodded, remembering the bags of clothes and shoes they purchased for only a dollar at the thrift store three blocks away from their home. They had been lucky enough to find quite a few items that fit Clarissa perfectly, although they were worn and some needed to be mended. She wondered again if she'd done the right thing. She hadn't given their real names to anyone. She was working for less than minimum wage in order to work without a Social Security number. She couldn't apply for welfare, because she didn't want anyone to be able to track them down. And, worst of all, she couldn't go to a free clinic to get her prescriptions because she was afraid Gary Copper knew about her disease and would somehow be able to trace her medical information and find them. She sighed, took Clarissa's hand, and together they walked down the hall toward the recreation room where dozens of elderly patients sat in chairs or wheelchairs.

She sent up a little prayer for forgiveness before they went through the large double doors and then smiled down at Clarissa and they both went inside.

Joyce, the Activity Director, a large woman with a warm and friendly smile, crossed the room to greet them.

"Hello, it's so nice of you to visit us again," she said. "Now help me remember your names again."

Clarissa smiled up at her. "I'm Clarissa..." she paused, making sure to remember their new last name, "Newman and this is my mom, Becca Newman."

"Wow, aren't you a smart young lady," Joyce replied. "I don't know if I mentioned this last time you came, but ten o'clock is the time we have to give all of our patients their medicine. So, it's a little crazy here."

"Oh, I'm sorry," Becca said. "I believe you might have said that. Are we in the way? Could Clarissa still sing to some of the residents?"

Joyce nodded. "Oh, of course," she said. "We just won't be able to help you very much. We're all needed to distribute the meds."

"Well, if we need you, I'll just poke my head out and find someone," Becca said. "Come on, Clarissa, let's have you stand over there by the aquarium."

Becca guided Clarissa over to a group of residents sitting near a large tropical aquarium.

"Are you my granddaughter?" an elderly woman in a wheelchair asked Clarissa.

"No," she responded, shaking her head. "But I don't have a grandma, so we could pretend."

The woman cackled with delight. "I'd like that just fine. You can call me Mami Nadja, that's Grandma Nadja from where I come from."

"Mami Nadja," Clarissa repeated.

"Very good," Mami replied. "So, what are you doing here with all us old people?"

"I came to sing to you," Clarissa said. "Is that okay?"

"What did you say?" a white-haired man lying in a recliner asked.

"She's going to sing to us, Charlie," Mami yelled. "Pay attention."

"I don't sing very well, but I could try," Charlie replied.

"Charlie, turn up your hearing aids," she yelled in response.

"They is turned up," Charlie yelled back. "They just ain't in my ears."

Mami rolled her eyes and winked at Clarissa, who giggled in response.

"Well, for goodness sake, man, stick them in your ears," she said.

Charlie positioned his hearing aids in his ears and turned to Clarissa. "Now, what did you say you were going to do?" he asked.

Her smile widened. "I'm going to sing to you," she said. "I learned lots of songs in school and from listening to the radio. Can I sing to you now?"

"Well, certainly, you go right ahead," Charlie encouraged.

Becca bent down and whispered into Clarissa's ear. "You go ahead and start, sweetheart. I have to find a bathroom, but I'll be right back."

Becca let herself out of the door in the back of the recreation room, the door that led to the residents' rooms. She walked purposely, as if she belonged there and was just visiting a family member. She greeted those passing by with a friendly nod, although her heart was hammering in her ears.

Knowing it was not uncommon for family members to visit the home on Sunday, Becca has purposely chosen Sunday to allow Clarissa to sing. She wanted a day with enough activity to hide the real purpose of her visit, because she knew if she was caught she could be sent to jail.

She came to the first hallway and cautiously examined the corridor. Halfway down was an unsupervised medicine trolley; the nurse was probably in a nearby room with a patient. Becca hurried down the hall, peeking into the rooms to try and find the nurse. She approached the cart before she found the nurse and quickly glanced at the containers, looking for the familiar orange hue of the theophylline. After a cursory examination, she realized her much needed pills were not on this cart.

"Yes, Mr. Frazier, I'll tell the director what you said," the nurse called as she walked out of the door just three feet away from Becca.

Becca's heart caught in her throat and she stepped away from the trolley, trying to come up with an explanation of why she was hovering near the medications. The nurse's hand was on the outside of the door when the room's occupant called out.

"What is that, Mr. Frazier?" the nurse asked, walking back into the room.

Becca breathed a sigh of relief and headed back up to the main hub to access the next hallway.

As she came toward the nurse's' station, the soft music that had been playing over the intercom was replaced with the urgent message that a Code Blue was taking place in room 143 W and all available personnel needed to respond.

Becca stepped into a small supply alcove and watched the nurses and staff jog down the hall in the direction of the room. A moment later, she stepped out and walked toward the vacated station.

From previous visits, Becca knew the pharmaceuticals were stored in a room directly behind the nurses' station. In the past she'd only been able to take a few pills, that only lasted several days or a week at the most if she took them judiciously. But if she was able to take them from storage, rather than the carts, she could get enough to last for much longer.

She looked up and down the hall and, seeing no one, slipped behind the counter. Watching the halls in front of the station, she slowly walked backward, toward the storage room. With her hands behind her back, she grasped hold of the doorknob and turned.

Unlocked!

She quickly slipped through the opened door and hurried into the small room. The shelves were loaded with medications, all arranged in alphabetical order and then by prescription strength. Tracing the names on the shelves with her finger, she finally came to the theophylline. The case was filled with the bright orange capsules – she couldn't believe her luck. She reached up and opened the case, grabbing several months' worth of pills and stuffed them into her pants' pockets. Then she reached up to get one more packet.

"Thank you, God," she breathed quietly.

"I don't think God has anything to do with thieves," said the voice behind her as the door closed with a click.

Chapter Nine

"Twinkle, twinkle, little star, how I wonder what you are," Clarissa held the last word of the song for a moment and then bowed to the applause throughout the room.

She took a deep breath and was about to start another song when Mami stopped her. "Clarissa, dear, I need your help for a few moments," she said. "Would you please push me to my room? I seem to have forgotten my medicine."

Knowing how important her mother's medicine was to her well-being, Clarissa didn't hesitate. She walked around the wheelchair, grasped the handles and pushed it forward. "Where do you want me to go?" she asked.

"Just through those doors," Mami said, pointing in the same direction Becca had taken a few minutes earlier. "And then turn to the left."

A nurse rushed past them pushing an empty gurney down the hall, but other than that, there were no other staff in the hall. Clarissa guided Mami carefully, making sure she avoided bumping her against the wall or any other objects in the hall.

"You are a good girl," Nadja said. "Your mother must be proud of you."

"She's proud of me and I'm proud of her too," Clarissa responded.

"And how long has it been since you had to run away and hide?"

Clarissa stopped pushing for a moment. "How did you know…?"

"Ah, draguta, you have no need to worry. I am not going to give you away, I want to help you."

Clarissa looked slowly around them, making sure there was no one who could hear her. "There's a bad man who's trying to take me away from my mommy," she explained in a lowered voice. "He killed my daddy, so we have to hide."

"And this bad man, do you know who he is?" Mami asked.

Clarissa shook her head. "Mommy says he has lots of money and he wants to take me away," she said. "He wants me for his daughter, even though Mommy and Daddy 'dopted me."

Mami pondered the child's words for a moment and then nodded. "Well, first we must help your mother," she said. "And then we will see what we can do next."

"Help Mommy?" Clarissa asked.

Mami nodded and pointed to the nurse's' station, only a few feet away. "Just push me over there," she said, "and then I want you to knock on that door, as hard as you can."

Once they reached the desk, Clarissa hurried to the door, closed her hand into a fist and pounded. The door opened and the head nurse stuck her head out. "What is it?" she asked curtly.

Clarissa stepped back, several feet away from the door. "I'm sorry…" she stammered.

"Don't frighten the child, Alicia," Mami said. "She was just doing me a favor."

The startled nurse turned toward Mami. "Oh, I'm sorry, I didn't realize…"

"No need for apologies, I don't have time to listen to you blather," Mami replied sternly. "I sent this girl's mother to either find some help or get me my medicine because I wasn't able to breathe properly. We came out to see what's taken her so long."

Clarissa looked back at Mami in surprise. She wasn't acting like the sweet grandma she had just helped down the hall. She was more like the principal at her school.

"You sent her?" Alicia asked.

"Of course I did," Mami replied. "Do you think I could go and get my own medicine? I tried to have someone on staff help me, but they were all busy."

"We had a Code Blue in the west wing," Alicia explained.

"Well, I'm sorry to hear that," Mami replied. "But I still need my medicine. Have you seen this little girl's mother? Did she get my medicine?"

Alicia turned back into the small room. "Did Mami send you in here for her medicine?" she asked.

"Excuse me, Alicia," Mami said, rolling her wheelchair behind the desk and up to the door. "Are you doubting my word?"

"Well, not really…"

"If you don't believe me, why don't you look and see what she's holding in her hand," Mami insisted. "Theophylline for my breathing problems."

The nurse marched forward, snatched the packet of pills from Becca's hand and read the label. "Why didn't you tell me you were helping one of the residents?" she snapped.

Becca took a deep breath, her face still pale and her eyes wide with fear. "Well, I…" she began.

"I doubt you gave her a chance to speak," Mami interrupted. "Now, can we finish with the interrogation and let Mrs. Newman give me the medicine I need? Or shall I pass out and then have an investigation into why I wasn't given my medicine in a timely manner?"

"No, of course not," Alicia stammered. "But I have to check your chart before I allow you to take it."

"Of course," Mami replied. "Please check it and then you will apologize to Mrs. Newman because she was just trying to help."

The nurse hurried past Nadja and her wheelchair and typed into the computer at the desk. After a few moments, she looked up and nodded. "I apologize, Mrs. Newman, it seems that Mami indeed needed her theophylline. In the future, however, I must insist that you do not take it upon yourself to get drugs for our residents. You are not authorized to do so and you could be jailed for the unlawful distribution of pharmaceuticals."

Becca nodded. "I'm sorry," she whispered, her voice dry. "I will never do it again, I assure you."

Becca handed Mami the packet of pills and the old woman looked up at her and smiled. "I believe I would be much more comfortable taking them in my room," she announced. "Would you mind pushing me there, Clarissa?"

Clarissa slid around from the other side of the nurses' desk, where she'd been hiding. "I can push you wherever you want to go."

Mami smiled. "Thank you, draguta, just push me up this aisle," she said, pointing to the hallway on the left. "Becca, please join us. I want to get to know you and your lovely daughter better."

In a few moments they were in Mami's room which was decorated in rich, vibrant colors and was filled with beautiful dark wood furniture and upholstered chairs of rich brocade.

"This doesn't look like a nursing home room," Becca said as they entered.

Mami laughed. "Oh, no," she said. "When it was decided I would live here, there were certain things that I was not going to do without. My furniture was one of them."

She rolled further into the room and then slowly lifted herself out of the wheelchair. Grasping the edges of a bookcase, she made her way to an ornate dresser and opened the top drawer. Reaching in, she pulled out a plastic bag filled with more orange pills.

"I noticed you collected some of these the first time you came," she said, pulling out the bag and handing it to Becca. "So, I placed them on my medications list and have been saving them for you for a few months."

Becca was astonished. "You knew...you saw?"

Mami smiled at her and patted her hand. "I saw a woman protecting her child," she said. "That's all."

"What? What do you know about us?" Becca asked.

"I know that you and Clarissa are not who you seem and that you are running away from someone who threatens to take her away from you."

Becca shook her head and stuffed the pills into her purse. "I'm very thankful for the pills," she said, her voice shaking. "And I can never thank you enough for what you did for me, for us, today. But we have to go now."

"But Mommy, Mami Nadja was going to help us," Clarissa protested. "She knew we were running away and hiding."

Becca's eyes widened. "Please, I beg of you, don't tell him," she said, fear evident in her voice.

"Oh, no, I wasn't going to tell..." Mami began.

Becca gripped Clarissa's hand and pulled her across the room. "We have to go," she said firmly.

"But I was going to..." Mami paused and sighed when the two slipped out of the room and her door was pulled firmly closed behind them. "Ah, Nadja, you dinlo, you spoke too soon and frightened them."

Chapter Ten

Ian walked down the stairs in the early morning, pulling his sweatshirt over his head. As he neared the kitchen he could smell the aroma of blueberry muffins. "Is Rosie already here?" he asked, as his head popped out of the neckline.

"Excuse me, Rosie is not the only one who can cook around here," Mary replied, from her position behind the kitchen counter.

The mixer was filled with buttery-colored batter with large plump blueberries throughout it. But the counter, sink and Mary's body also had their share of batter covering them.

"Was there a war then?" Ian asked casually, as he picked up a dish towel and wiped some of the batter off Mary's nose.

"No," she sighed. "I just didn't realize how powerful the 'High' setting was on the mixer. It was like jet propulsion, batter flying everywhere."

She pushed back her hair, only to find a glob of batter hanging from it. "Gross!"

"And how did the survivors turn out?" he asked as he reached over and picked up a cooked muffin from a basket at the end of the counter, unwrapped it and took a very small tentative bite.

"Oh, that was rude," Mary said. "It's not going to kill you."

He grinned and took a bigger bite. "Well, what a pleasant surprise, these are quite good," he said.

"Well, if there was ever something known as Scottish charm, it skipped a generation with you," Mary said.

Ian grabbed another muffin. "Ach, no, it's not the Scottish who are charming," he said. "We're the warriors. We let the Irish be the charming ones."

"How lucky for the Scottish women," Mary replied acerbically.

Winking at her, Ian laughed. "Oh, darling, women much prefer fine braw warriors to warm them at night."

He bit into the second muffin with enthusiasm.

"So, how are they?" Mary asked.

His filled mouth prevented him from answering directly, and he took a moment to really observe Mary. She will still dressed in her sweats, her favorite pajamas, and was wearing an apron. Her hair was still sleep mussed and she looked worried.

"They are the finest examples of blueberry muffins I've ever eaten," he replied and watched the rosy glow spread across her face. "And as long as you promise not to tell, I'd say there were better than Rosie's."

Her beaming smile was reward enough for his slight white lie. "And how long have you been working to perfect this wee morsel of delight?" he asked.

Drooping her shoulders, she let out a weary sigh. "That's the third try," she confessed. "I kept leaving things out or doing things wrong. Who would have thought baking was so tricky?"

Smiling gently at her, he wiped a little more batter from her hair. "Well, they're all the more delicious for the effort," he said. "And now, would you want me to tidy the kitchen and bake a few more batches while you run upstairs and shower?"

"Who says Scots can't be charming?" she asked. "Thank you."

"Ach, my pleasure," he said, grabbing another muffin from the basket.

"But don't eat all the muffins," she called from the stairs.

His mouth filled, he mumbled after her, "Don't worry, darling, I won't eat them all."

Twenty minutes later, it was Mary's turn to come jogging down the stairs and enjoy the aroma of fresh-baked muffins. The kitchen was neat and tidy and there was a heaping pile of still-warm muffins in the cloth-lined basket.

"Thank you, Ian," she said. "Everything looks great."

"Aye, and you owe me a greater favor than you think," he replied. "Thanks to you I'll be working out for several hours today to work off all the carbs your wily muffins tempted me to eat."

"How many?" she asked, trying, but not succeeding in hiding a grin.

"Ach, I ate ten of them," he said, rubbing his stomach. "I just couldn't help myself."

Her smile widened and she stepped up and placed a kiss on his cheek. "That's one of the nicest things anyone has ever said to me."

He shook his head and winked at her. "Crazy women."

The door opened as Ian spoke and Stanley walked inside behind Rosie. "Who's crazy?" he asked.

"Women are crazy," Ian repeated, joining Mary as they went to the door to greet them.

"I can agree with you on that," Stanley said, grumbling more than usual.

"Stanley!" Rosie chided, her normal cheery disposition absent. "Women are not crazy."

Mary looked at both of her friends carefully. "Is there something going on?" she asked. "You both seem awfully tense."

Stanley shrugged. "I didn't get much sleep last night," he said, "that's all."

Rosie nodded. "Same here, it was a restless night."

Grinning, Ian gave Stanley a soft punch on the arm. "Why Stanley you old rascal…" he began.

"Tweren't nothing like that, so get your mind out of the gutter," Stanley interrupted. "Rosie was at her house and I was at my house. And I'm sure what kept me tossing and turning was nothing like what kept Rosie up."

71

Rosie glared at him. "How do you know what kept me up?"

"I ain't saying I know and I ain't saying I don't," he said. "But what kept me up was so far out of the ordinary, I doubt anyone else would have experienced it."

Shaking her head, Rosie turned to face him. "Well, what kept me up was also out of the ordinary," she replied. "Quite out of the ordinary."

"What kept you both up?" Mary asked.

"Ghosts!" they shouted simultaneously.

"Ghosts?" they asked, turning to each other.

"You saw a ghost?" Rosie asked Stanley.

"Didn't exactly see it," he said. "But something was there for sure."

She nodded. "Yes, for me too," she said. "In my bedroom."

"Well, I'm sure there's some explanation," Ian said. "It's certainly strange that you are both having similar experiences."

"I wonder if it's the same ghost, visiting both of you," Mary said. "We could investigate…"

"Investigate what?" Bradley asked, coming through the front door. "Hey, are those blueberry muffins I smell?"

Bradley bypassed the group in the living room and headed straight into the kitchen. He picked up a muffin and took a bite. "Oh, Rosie, these are heavenly," he said. "Stanley is a lucky man."

Mary turned away from him, disappointed. "So, why don't you tell me about the ghosts," she said to Stanley and Rosie. She led them into the front room so they could sit on the couch.

Ian walked over to Bradley, who was helping himself to a second muffin. "You big dolt," he whispered. "Mary was up at the wee hours of the morning making the muffins."

Bradley's eyes widened. "Mary made these?" he asked. "Why didn't she say something?"

"I'm guessing because the person she made them for immediately assumed someone else made them," Ian pointed out.

"I'm an idiot."

Ian nodded. "Aye, you are. But even an idiot has a chance at redemption."

Bradley put the half-eaten muffin on the table and walked into the front room where Mary sat on a chair across from Stanley and Rosie. He knelt down in front of her.

"You made the muffins," he said.

She shrugged and nodded, turning her head away and not meeting his eyes. "No big deal," she muttered.

"Stand up," he said, as he stood up too.

She looked up at him. "What?"

"Stand up," he repeated.

Shaking her head in confusion, she slowly stood up in front of him. "What?"

Moving quickly, he lifted Mary into his arms and started walking toward the door.

"What are you doing?" Mary cried, half-heartedly pushing at his shoulders.

"Grab your coat and your purse, Mary, I'm taking you to Vegas today," he said. "I could barely wait until June to marry you when you were just the love of my life, but now that I know how well you can bake… Well, I know your parents will be disappointed, but there is no putting this off."

She giggled. "You big goof, we are not going to Vegas today."

Rosie laughed. "You just have to be back before Friday for our wedding," she called.

"And you probably won't be finding a bridal suite that includes a kitchen," Ian said. "You're better off staying here."

"Please Mary," Bradley grinned down at her, placed a kiss on her lips and whispered. "That was even better than the muffins. And the muffins were amazing."

She shook her head and smiled at him. "You're forgiven for thinking Rosie made the muffins," she said, bringing his face down to hers for another kiss.

He deepened the kiss for a moment and then placed his forehead against hers. "I love you, Mary O'Reilly," he whispered.

"I love you back," she said.

Mary's cell phone rang and Ian handed it to her. Her eyes still brimming with laughter and love, she answered it. "Good morning," she called into the phone. "Hi, Sean. Did you get the information I sent you about Henry Madison? Yeah, we're pretty sure he was another one of Gary Copper's victims."

Then the laughter left her face. "Oh, of course, I'll tell him. Yes, we'll be there. First thing in the morning. Yes, I know the place. Thanks, Sean. Love you too. Bye."

Bradley slowly put her down on the floor. "What is it?" he asked.

"They are going to arraign Gary Copper tomorrow and Sean wants us all to be there," she said.

Rosie hurried across the room and put her arms around Mary. "Are you ready to see him again?" she asked. "You have only just started to not react..."

Nodding, Mary returned the hug. "I'll be fine," she said. "I have to be fine. There's no way that man in going to walk free again."

Ian tossed Bradley another muffin. "Well, then, let's have a sit down and discuss our plans," he said. "Bradley did you get Henry's information?"

Bradley nodded. "I've sent a request for a copy of his autopsy," he said. "I'll get it later this week."

"Who's Henry?" Stanley asked.

"The man who was raising my daughter," Bradley explained. "We think Gary Copper killed him too."

"Oh, my dear, Bradley, that's horrible," Rosie said. "What can we do to help?"

"Wait, what about your ghosts?" Mary asked.

"Oh, well perhaps it was a one-time thing," Rosie said. "Nothing to get worried about."

Stanley nodded. "Yeah, I probably imagined it. We got more important things to do."

"Are you sure?" Ian asked.

"If I get another visitor, you'll be the first to know," Rosie assured him.

"Okay, well we do have a lot of catching up to do," Ian said. "And I would suggest we get a move on."

Chapter Eleven

The small home on Freeport's north side was showing gentle signs of neglect. The porch was scattered with faded sales flyers, plastic-wrapped telephone books and dried autumn leaves. The front steps still held remnants from the snowfall several days ago and there was a crack in one of the front windows from a thrown rock, the culprit still sitting on the sill.

"I'm so glad Katie had an extra key," Mary said as they stood in front of the empty house.

"I still think it's strange she would just leave," Ian said. "This is where she's made her roots."

"When you feel helpless, the first thing you consider is running away," Bradley said. "If she really had no one left, being lost in a crowd is a lot easier."

Mary, Bradley and Ian made their way up the stairs and to the front door. Bradley took the key out of his pocket and inserted it into the lock. The door opened easily and they walked through the small hallway into the living room.

Sunlight illuminated the dust motes that lingered in the middle of the room. There was an overstuffed sofa in a floral design against one wall and a matching love seat next to it. A small bookcase of children's books sat next to the loveseat, several books were still open with favorite pages exposed.

Mary walked over and picked one up. "This was one of my favorite books," she said. "It's all about a little bird who's trying to find her mother."

"Fairly ironic," Ian said, looking over her shoulder.

"No, not at all," Bradley said from across the room.

He was standing in front of a tall dark bookshelf that was divided into cubbyholes. In the center cubby was a small framed photo of a man, woman and a little girl, all smiling widely into the camera. "She looks like she wasn't searching for anything," he said, lifting the frame from the shelf and studying it more closely. "She looks like she was happy and secure."

Mary and Ian walked over and looked at the photo.

"Aye, she's happy. You can see it in her eyes," Ian said. "But there's no denying who her parents really are."

"She looks like Jeannine, but she has your eyes," Mary said softly.

He took a deep shuddering breath. "She's my daughter," he said, his voice cracking. "There's no doubt in my mind. Clarissa is my little girl."

Ian looked over Bradley's shoulder. "She's yours alright," he said. "And it's a blessing she didn't get your nose."

Surprised laughter slipped through his lips and eased the tension that had been building inside his body. He took a deep breath and put the photo back on the shelf. "Well, let's get to work finding her," he said.

Mary reached up, took the photo off the shelf and handed it to Bradley. "I think it would be fine for you to keep this," she said, putting her hand up when he began to protest. "If for nothing else, it will be helpful to show people when we are searching for her."

He didn't say anything for a moment, just nodded and slid the photo into his coat pocket. "Thank you," he said, his voice tight with emotion, "thank you both for your help."

"What's to thank?" Ian asked with a casual shrug. "All for one and all that."

Mary smiled softly. "Yeah, what he said," she added, reaching up and kissing Bradley. "Now let's find Clarissa."

They walked through the first floor searching through desks drawers and cabinets for any more information that would help them find out where they'd gone. "Uh, oh," Ian said, holding a small piece of paper in his hand. "The mother, Becca, is on theophylline."

"What does that mean?" Mary asked.

"It means she has some kind of respiratory disease," he replied. "And by the small dosage, she's using it to maintain open airways – I would guess her lungs are deteriorating."

"So, she's trying to take care of a child in Chicago while she's sick?" Bradley asked. "How did she even think she could do this?"

"Who's in Chicago and what are you doing in my house?" a deep male voice demanded.

Both Mary and Ian turned toward the voice, but Bradley continued to search. Mary stepped over to Bradley and took his hand. "We have company," she whispered to him.

He turned to see the ghost of a tall, muscular man dressed in work clothes standing in the doorway. "You're the father," Bradley exclaimed, "from the photo. You're Clarissa's father, Henry."

"You know my daughter? Where is she? What have you done with Clarissa and Becca?"

The ghost raced across the room and hovered threateningly in front of Bradley. "Tell me what you've done with my wife and daughter," he demanded. "Tell me where you've taken them."

"You really love her," Bradley said, some of the tension in his heart easing.

"Of course I do," Henry exclaimed. "I'm her father."

Bradley nodded. "Yes, you are," he said calmly. "And I'm her father too."

Henry shook his head. "Are you some kind of nut case? Are you like that dentist? Clarissa doesn't need more than one father, and that job has been taken by me. Now, where have you taken them?"

"We don't have your wife or your daughter," Mary replied. "We're here to find out what happened to them too."

He shook his head. "Someone's taken them," he said. "Becca would have never left without me. I came home and they were gone. I've been searching for them ever since."

Ian moved forward. "Henry, I'm Ian," he said. "And this is Mary O'Reilly, a private investigator and this fellow you think is a nut is actually Police Chief Bradley Alden."

Henry turned to Bradley. "You're a cop?" he asked.

Bradley nodded.

"Good! It's about time you guys showed up," he said. "We've got to find my wife, she's sick. If she runs out of pills…"

Ian held up the prescription form. "She runs out of air," he finished.

Henry nodded. "She has COPD, she's not supposed to be stressed," he said. "I was taking care of her, of both of them…"

"Aye, I understand you were," Ian said, "and doing a fine job of it. We're friends of the Brennans and they told us how devoted you've been to your family."

"That's how…that's how you know my name?" he asked.

"We know quite a bit about you, Henry," Mary said. "Like how you went to see Dr. Gary Copper to ask him to leave your family alone."

Henry nodded. "Yes, I went to see him and he agreed to leave us be," he said.

"Did he give you anything to eat or drink while you were there?" Ian asked.

"Yes, he insisted I try his sweet tea. And I was trying to get him to see reason, so I did," Henry replied. "It actually was pretty bad, had a funny after-taste to it."

"I bet," Bradley said. "Copper was known for his bad after-taste."

"Henry, do you remember what happened after you left Dr. Copper's house?" Mary asked.

Pausing, Henry searched his memory. "I got in my car," he said slowly. "I drove back to the highway…I was feeling a little weird, like the tea didn't sit right. But I had to get to work…"

He stopped and he looked at Mary. "I can't remember anything after that. I only remember I got home and everyone was gone."

He glided up to Mary. "Did he take them?" he demanded. "Did Copper take them?"

Mary shook her head and met Henry's eyes. "No, Becca was concerned that he would come, so she took Clarissa and ran away," she explained.

"But why didn't she wait for me?" he asked.

"Because Copper poisoned you," she said slowly. "He poisoned your sweet tea. On the way home from Sycamore the tea made you pass out and you crashed your car. Henry, you died on the way back to Freeport."

Henry slowly shook his head. "No. No. I'm not dead," he argued. "I'm here, I'm right here in front of you. Why are you doing this? I can't be dead. I need to take care of Becca and Clarissa. They need me. I promised them."

His voice cracked and he fell to his knees. Dropping his head in his hands, he cried, "I can't be dead. Who is going to help them?"

Bradley knelt down next to him, making sure he had Mary's hand securely in his own. "We will, Henry," he promised. "We'll find them and we'll help them. But we're going to need you to help us."

Henry looked up and met Bradley's eyes. "You don't understand," he whispered, grief evident in his voice. "Becca doesn't have much time. But she didn't know... I made the doctor promise not to tell her. She was so worried about not being there for us, I didn't want her last months to be focused on the end."

"How long did the doctor think she had?" Ian asked.

Henry shook his head, his eyes filled with grief. "A year, maybe two," he replied and as he watched their reaction he asked, "Why?"

"It's March, Henry," Mary said. "You've been dead for nearly a year."

His eyes widened and he shook his head. "You have to find my little girl."

He floated to the middle of the room. "Clarissa," he called out. "Where are you?"

Then he faded away.

Chapter Twelve

"Do you want me to walk you up to Mrs. Gunderson's apartment, dear?" Becca asked Clarissa as she closed their apartment door.

Clarissa shook her head. Not only did she not want her mother to have to climb the extra stairs, she certainly didn't want her mother to see the kind of apartment Mrs. Gunderson lived in. If she did, she would be worried all the time, and her mother did not need another thing to worry about.

"I'm fine, Mommy," she replied. "I love walking up the stairs by myself."

Becca bent over and kissed Clarissa's forehead. "Do you have your key?" she asked.

Clarissa pulled the chain from under her shirt and showed her mother the key.

"You let Mrs. Gunderson use that when she brings you downstairs and tucks you in," her mother reminded her. "You understand."

Clarissa nodded obediently, knowing that Mrs. Gunderson generally kicked her out of the apartment at about seven o'clock, two hours before she was supposed to, because her shows were on television and she didn't want to be disturbed. Clarissa generally spent the last several hours alone in their apartment, sitting in the darkened room, so no one would know she was there.

"I will, Mommy," she said. "I promise."

Becca looked up the stairs, guilt and anguish filling her heart. She didn't want to leave Clarissa alone with anyone, but she had to go to work. They needed her income.

"Okay, darling, I won't be late and I'll try to bring some dessert home this time."

"Thanks, Mommy, I love you."

"I love you too, sweetheart."

Clarissa stepped up one step and turned and watched her mother slowly struggle down the steps to finally let herself out the front door into the cold afternoon. Sighing, Clarissa turned and walked up the stairs to the fourth floor and Mrs. Gunderson.

The stairwell was dark and it smelled bad. Clarissa tried to avoid touching the railing because it was often sticky and once, when she had been holding on to it, something crawled over her hand. The walls were stained and littered with graffiti, words that Clarissa's mother had told her were not nice. And very often the stairs were covered with garbage from the apartments above them.

Clarissa kicked a beer bottle out of the way and heard it clatter all the way down the stairs behind her. When she reached the fourth floor, she walked to the fifth apartment down the hall.

Her stomach clenched as she heard the yelling coming from within the apartment. Mrs. Gunderson's husband was home, because it was Sunday. She sighed, and then, with reluctance, knocked on the door.

"Who the hell is knocking on the damn door?" she heard Mr. Gunderson yell.

"Probably that little brat from downstairs," Mrs. Gunderson replied, her voice even louder than her husband's. "If you had a decent job I wouldn't have to watch some whore's kid."

"Yeah, well you could get a real job yourself," he yelled back, "instead of sitting on your fat ass all day watching TV."

Another door opened on the floor above them. "You give me that money, hear?" she heard a man call out. "You give me the money or you give me back that blow."

"I ain't got no money, man," a woman argued back. "And I need my stuff. So, you back away from the door or I will cut you."

"Bitch! Give me my money!" the man screamed.

She knocked on the door again, urgently.

"Answer the damn door," Mr. Gunderson yelled.

The door flew open in front of Clarissa and Mrs. Gunderson reached out and grabbed her by her shoulder and pulled her into the house. "Didn't your momma ever teach you any manners?" she yelled, slapping Clarissa across the face. "You don't pound on people's doors; you wait for them to answer."

"Yes, ma'am," Clarissa answered, reeling from the sting of the slap.

Mrs. Gunderson pulled Clarissa down through the apartment into a small room off the kitchen. It was a little larger than a closet and was filled with stacked boxes. There was a small, child-sized table in one corner with a bowl of broken crayons and a stack of scrap paper on it.

"Now, you go in there and color," she said. "And don't make no noise. We don't want to be interrupted. Shouldn't have to be watching you on Sunday, no how. Just doing it out of the goodness of my heart."

Clarissa nodded. "Yes, ma'am," she repeated.

The woman relented a little. "You hungry?" she asked. "I got some peanut butter."

Clarissa glanced behind her, to the dirty kitchen counter and tried not to shudder as she watched a cockroach crawl across the jar of peanut butter. "No, thank you," she replied. "We just ate before I came."

"Well, good, 'cause I ain't s'posed to feed you no ways," she said. "And you gotta go home a little early tonight. Me and Mr. Gunderson, we got some plans for tonight."

Clarissa nodded.

"And you don't tell your momma I let you go down early," she said. "We both know you's a big girl and can take care of yourself. Right?"

Clarissa nodded again.

"And don't you let your momma forget, I get my pay for next month tomorrow. I can't watch you 'cept I get my pay in advance. I ain't gonna have no one cheat me."

"I'll bring it tomorrow," Clarissa promised.

"Effie, the damn show is on pause, are you going to get in here?" Mr. Gunderson yelled.

"Shut the hell up, Lee, I'm taking care of the kid," she yelled back.

Clarissa moved into the little room and obediently sat at the table. "I'll be back in an hour to let you out, case you need to go potty or something," Mrs. Gunderson replied, before she closed the door and Clarissa could hear the lock click on the door.

She pulled a piece of paper across the table, picked out a blue crayon and began to draw a pair of large wings.

Chapter Thirteen

Rosie locked up her house for the night and finally made her way to her bedroom. She flipped on the overhead light and bathed the room in brightness. Then she picked up the remote from the nightstand and turned on a news channel, so there was noise in the room. She hurried over to her bathroom and quickly completed her evening rituals and then made her way to her bed.

Her eyes were continually drawn to the closet door. Was it still closed or had it opened just a bit?

Even when she was in the bathroom, she kept looking into the mirror, watching the door. Expecting it to open on its own. A shudder slid down her spine and she wrapped her arms around herself. "Okay, Rosie, get a grip," she lectured herself. "You've lived in this house for over ten years. You love this house. Nothing is going to hurt you."

Taking a deep breath, she turned off the light in the bathroom and made her way into her bedroom. The noise from the television was comforting. She even got enough nerve to walk to the closet door and test it; to be sure it was shut.

She released a sigh of relief when the door was firm, and began to walk to her bed when she heard a slight click. *Did something just turn the knob?*

She turned quickly and faced the door, her heart pounding. She stared at the door, willing it to open, but praying it would not.

After a few moments, she moved back, away from the door toward her bed. Pausing halfway across the room, she walked over to her chaise lounge. Moving behind it, she pushed it across the room until it was in front of the closet door. She pushed it further, so it was jammed up against the door. "That ought to keep the door closed," she said, brushing her hands together.

She didn't turn off the overhead light until she had flipped on the lamp on her nightstand. Then she walked across the room to turn it off. The room was still fairly bright with the pictures from the television program, but the lamp made her feel even more secure.

Climbing into bed, the television and the lamp still on, she slid underneath the blankets. Her night mask stayed on the nightstand, unused. She didn't want to be that vulnerable. Purposely positioning herself away from the closet, she pulled the blankets up as high as she could, cocooning herself inside them.

Lying in bed, listening to the sounds of her house, she tensed at every creak and bump. Finally, after about twenty minutes, she allowed herself to relax. Her eyes began to drift shut and the tension began to slowly slip away. She could feel herself being drawn into sleep and she welcomed it. Just as she was drifting away, she heard the knob on the closet turn.

Immediately awake, her heart beating in her throat, she listened as the chaise lounge was pushed forward on the floor. She couldn't move. Almost couldn't breathe. She was paralyzed with fear. She gripped the blankets tightly until her knuckles where white and waited. The television turned off and the light on the nightstand darkened. Then she felt the bed give way and knew that something was beside her on the bed.

She felt nausea roll in her stomach and her heart pounded in her chest. She could feel the darkness of whatever was in the room with her. Her legs were numb; her voice was dry in her throat. She couldn't even scream. She felt it move closer to her in the bed.

Pressing her eyes together, she gripped the blankets even tighter and did the only thing she could think of. She prayed. "Dear God, Please help me. I'm so frightened. Please make this thing go away."

She felt the mattress shift, felt the presence lift away from her and finally, after a few moments, heard the closet door close. After what seemed to be an eternity, she could lower the blanket. Her bedroom was back the way it had been before she had gone to bed. The chaise was still against the closet door. The television was still running and the lamp was still on.

Biting her lower lip, she slowly shook her head. No, she hadn't imagined it. There was something in her room. Something on her bed.

Finally, she glanced down to the side of her bed and trembled when she saw the depression in the blankets next to her. Wordlessly, her breath coming out in short gasps, she slid from under the covers. She ran across her room and into her living room. Grabbing her coat, she slipped it on as she grabbed her purse and her keys. There was no way she was going to spend another night in that house.

Chapter Fourteen

Stanley sat in the dark, a high-powered flashlight in his lap, and waited to see if any nocturnal visitors were going to pay him a call. "Come on, you lily-livered coward," he whispered, "show yourself."

The clock in the living room clicked with each passing second, echoing in the stillness of the night. He slowly scanned his house, from his vantage in his favorite recliner. A ray of light from the streetlamp outside slipped through the closed curtains and drew a narrow line across the middle of the carpet. Tiny dots of green and red from the instrument panel of the television and DVD player shone from the shelf of the TV stand. The digital clock light over the stovetop glowed a slightly iridescent green. But there were no other sources of light in the house.

He waited and watched. Finally, as the clock whirred on the hour and the chimes echoed eleven o'clock, he saw it. The hairs on the back of his neck stood straight up. A faint glow, the size of an adult, floated through the hall from his office to his bedroom. He felt his knees go weak, but forced himself to stand and silently follow; his flashlight in his hand.

He slipped around the kitchen counter and into the hallway. Sliding against the wall, he slowly made his way toward the open bedroom doorway. His hope that the glow was merely the reflection from passing car lights was immediately crushed when he saw it slowly moving back and forth in his bedroom. He stood in the doorway, his heart in his throat, his blood pounding in his temples and his eyes wide with shock.

The entity moved to his dresser and Stanley watched the top drawer slowly open. Items of clothing from the drawer were lifted up and thrown across the room; pairs of black socks landed on the bed, handkerchiefs were draped over the lampshade, t-shirts tossed on the chair and, finally, a pair of boxer shorts flew across the room and landed at Stanley's feet.

This can't be real, he thought. *I must have fallen asleep in the chair.*

He closed his eyes and slapped his cheek. *Wake up, Stanley!*

But when he opened his eyes, the boxers were still on the floor at his feet and his personal items were still being thrown across the room. He looked back to the drawer and saw the small framed photo he kept of his first wife levitating in the air. The frame was a fragile heirloom and would shatter if it were thrown haphazardly across his room. "Now hold on there," he called without thought, "you ain't throwing that nowhere."

The entity paused and allowed the frame to slowly drop back into the drawer. Then it turned and faced Stanley. He gasped in shock. Within the glowing light he was able to see a face, softly formed and wistful, the face of his dead wife stared back at him.

"Verna?" he called out tentatively. "That you Verna?"

A small translucent tear slipped down her cheek. She held her arms up toward him and nodded. And although her lips never moved, he could hear her whisper.

"Don't forget, Stanley. Don't forget."

And then she was gone.

Chapter Fifteen

Frantic pounding on the door and ringing of the bell had both Mary and Ian springing from their respective beds and meeting at the top of the stairs. "Who do you think it is?" Ian asked as they jogged down the steps.

Mary shrugged. "Most of my visitors don't knock."

Ian reached the door first and opened it. Rosie threw herself into his arms, sobbing. "There's something in my house," she cried, tears running down her face. "I can't go back there."

Ian led her into the front room and guided her to the couch. "It's okay, darling, you're safe now," he murmured. "There's no reason to be afraid."

She sat on the couch next to Ian. Mary tucked an afghan around her, sat on her other side and gave her a hug. "Do you want anything? A cup of tea? A glass of water?" she asked.

Rosie shook her head and took a few of the tissues Ian offered her. "No, no, I'm fine," she said, catching her breath and mopping her face. "You must think I'm a goose. It's just that I was so scared and didn't know where to go."

"Well of course you needed to come here," Ian said. "We're family."

Mary looked over Rosie's head and smiled at him. "Yes, we are family," she agreed. "Now, what frightened you?"

Taking a deep breath that caused her to shiver, Rosie waited for a moment and then began to speak. "For the past two nights I thought there was something in my room," she explained. "The closet door was open when I woke up and I know I closed it tightly. I can't sleep with the closet door open. Then, the feeling in my room, it was…darker. And when I woke up, there was a body-sized imprint in my bed right next to where I was sleeping."

"Are you sure…" Ian began.

She held up her hand and interrupted him. "Tonight I pretended to be asleep," she said. "I heard the closet door open and I felt someone get into my bed next to me."

"Rosie," Mary exclaimed.

"I lay there, terrified," she continued. "And then I realized the only thing I could do was pray. So, I did."

"And?" Ian asked.

"And it got off the bed and I heard the closet door close," she said, her voice trembling. "And then I jumped out of bed, grabbed my purse and my coat and came here."

Ian fell back against the couch and stroked his chin with his hand. "You know, Rosie, unless you want to abandon your home, you're going to have to go back," he said. "The longer you stay away, the more powerful this entity will become."

She turned to him. "So, you don't think I'm crazy?" she asked. "You believe me?"

Mary shook her head. "No, Rosie, we know you're not crazy," she replied. "There is something in your house. But you don't have to go back alone. We'll help you figure out who it is and how to get rid of it."

"Aye, and you don't have to go back tonight," Ian said. "Just give me a moment and I'll make up the bed in the guestroom for you."

"But, Ian, that's where you sleep," Rosie argued.

Ian shook his head. "Rosie, me darling, no arguing tonight," he replied, leaning over and placing a kiss on her cheek. "I'll be back in a trice."

Shaking her head, she turned to Mary. "I just can't believe this is happening," Rosie said. "Who in the world gets haunted the week before they are getting married?"

As he walked across the room, another frantic pounding on the door stopped him in his tracks. Ian walked to the door and opened it to find Stanley on the porch scowling at him.

"It's okay," Ian said. "She's fine, just a little shaken up."

"What the hell you talking about?" Stanley growled.

Ian cocked his head slightly to the side. "Why are you here, Stanley?"

"'Cause I got a gol-darned ghost haunting my house," he exclaimed. "And if that ain't bad enough, seems like it's my wife, Verna."

Ian shook his head and grinned. "Well, now, isn't that a coincidence," he said. "Sounds like Rosie's got some haunting issues too."

He stepped back and invited Stanley inside.

Rosie turned and looked over the back of the couch. "Stanley, how did you know?" she asked.

Stanley harrumphed and adjusted his trousers at the waist. "So, you get in trouble and you come knocking on Mary's door," he grumbled. "Seems like you oughtta been running to me for protection."

"And just where did you run to when you had a ghost issue?" Ian asked nonchalantly.

"Ain't the point," Stanley countered with a sniff.

Ian laughed. "Sit down, Stanley," he said. "I'll put a pot on and then we can all discuss your ghosts."

Chapter Sixteen

Mary tiptoed down the stairs and nearly jumped when Ian walked out of the kitchen. He put his finger to his lips and motioned with his head. "Stanley's still sleeping," he whispered.

Mary nodded and motioned to Ian to follow her back into the kitchen. "It was so nice of you to give Rosie your room," she said. "How did you sleep?"

Grimacing while rolling his neck, Ian picked up his cup of tea. "Well, your recliner is not the most comfortable of beds," he said. "But I'll survive."

"Yeah, thanks for giving Stanley the couch," she said.

Ian looked over toward the living room and rolled his eyes. "The way that man snores, I'm surprised any ghost would dare enter his bedroom," he replied. "We've got to get Stanley's ghost out of there if we're to be getting any sleep in this house."

Mary chuckled softly. "Well, I could hear him upstairs, so I'm sure it must have been shaking the walls down here."

"Waking the dead," Ian replied.

Laughing, Mary nodded. "And maybe that's the problem."

Ian grinned. "Aye, it could be. So, are you ready for what lies ahead of us today?"

She nodded. "As ready as I will ever be," she replied. "I'm wearing my power outfit."

Ian glanced at her navy blue suit, striped silk blouse and high heels and nodded with approval. "That'll do nicely," he said. "They'll not be able to shake you on the witness stand. You look like a strong and competent professional."

"Good, because I feel like a frightened and nervous fifth-grade girl," she admitted.

"And how do I look?" he asked, turning in a little semi-circle and sending her a wink over his shoulder.

It felt good to laugh, loosen the knots in her stomach. She really dreaded seeing Gary Copper again and feared, even more, what her reaction might be. "You look just fine," she finally said. "But…"

Ian turned back around to face her. "But?" he asked, one eyebrow raised.

"But, really, the black spandex shirt would have been better."

He laughed aloud and then immediately quieted his voice. "You are a tease, Mary O'Reilly," he said and then he put a comforting arm around her. "And you'll be fine. He's not a big bad boogieman, he's naught but a wee evil man and you already beat him once."

"Jeannine beat him," she replied.

"Jeannine beat him using your skills," he answered. "He's no match for you, remember that."

A loud snore interrupted their conversation and Mary placed a hand over her mouth to muffle her laughter. "Shall we wait for Bradley outside?" Mary finally asked.

"It's about ten degrees above zero out there," Ian replied.

Another snore vibrated the room. "Aye, what are we waiting for?" Ian asked, grabbing his coat.

"Lead the way."

They had just closed the door behind them when Bradley pulled up in the cruiser. Hurrying to the car, Mary slipped into the passenger seat and Ian sat in the back. Bradley leaned over and gave Mary a quick kiss. "Good timing," he said, "were you watching from the window?"

"No, we were escaping with our hearing intact," Ian replied.

"Excuse me?" Bradley asked.

"Stanley spent the night on the couch," Mary explained, "and he has a bit of a snoring issue."

"Aye, like the Titanic had a bit of a water issue," Ian said. "The man shakes the house with each breath."

Bradley smiled, put the cruiser in gear and pulled away from the curb. "Why did Stanley spend the night at your place?" he asked.

"He and Rosie have both had encounters with ghosts in their homes," Mary said. "Stanley thinks his dead wife is haunting him, but Rosie has no idea who is entering her bedroom at night."

"Her bedroom?" Bradley responded. "That would be creepy."

"Aye, especially when it decides to cozy up to her without her permission."

Bradley stopped at the corner more abruptly then he would have done under ordinary circumstances. "What the hell? It's getting into bed with her?" he asked. "Is she okay?"

"Yes, she's fine," Mary said. "She came to the house late last night and Ian gave up his room to her."

"Aye, the recliner is no place for a grown man to rest," Ian said.

Nodding, Bradley smiled. "You have my full sympathy."

He turned left onto South Street and headed toward Highway 20. "So what are we going to do about these ghosts?"

"We thought we'd check them out tonight," Mary replied, "see if we can figure out who they are and why they've suddenly appeared."

Bradley glanced over to her. "Do you have any suspicions? I mean, Stanley's wife appearing to him a week before he's supposed to marry Rosie sounds a little more like cold feet and a lot less like a cold grave."

"So you're thinking Stanley's insecurities about getting married again are manifesting themselves in the form of his dead wife?" Ian asked.

Bradley glanced at Ian through the rearview mirror and shrugged. "I probably wouldn't have put it exactly that way, but yes," he agreed. "He's nervous about getting married again and he starts seeing things."

"Actually, you have a fair point there," Ian agreed. "But there's also a chance that his dead wife might have been visiting him all along. And he just didn't see her."

Mary turned in her chair and looked at Ian. "I don't understand," she said. "Why would he suddenly be able to see her now?"

"Because of you," he replied. "I've done some research about ESP and someone's ability to see spirits and a great part of seeing is just believing you can do it. Most of us either don't want to see a ghost or don't believe we can. When we open ourselves up to the possibility, we release our minds to see what has often been there all along."

"Since Stanley and Rosie have been helping Mary, and you, with some of these cases," Bradley said, with a little skepticism in his voice, "you think their minds are more open to the possibility of ghosts, and so now they can see them? I don't know if I buy that one."

Ian leaned back in his seat and thought for a moment. "Okay, think about it this way," he suggested. "You've fallen in love with an extraordinary woman..."

Bradley turned and winked at Mary. "Yeah, I'm with you so far."

Chuckling, Ian continued. "And suddenly, everywhere you go you find connections. You go to the grocery store and see the peanut butter she keeps on her top shelf and you stop and grin at the jar for a few moments before you catch yourself, shake your head and move on down the aisle."

Smiling widely, Mary turned to Ian. "Really?"

Bradley glanced up into the mirror again and met Ian's eyes. "You've been spying on me," he said.

Ian grinned. "Aye, I saw you in the market the other day," he confessed. "If I didn't know the truth, I would have thought you loony for sure."

"Thanks, Ian," Bradley remarked. "But that doesn't…"

"Aye, it does," he interrupted. "Suddenly, because of your relationship to her, your mind is looking for connections. Her scent, her walk, the color of her hair. Your mind is cataloging and sorting all kinds of new information because you're in love with Mary. Think about it."

Bradley was silent for a few moments and then he nodded. "Okay, I admit I'm a little obsessed with anything Mary, but what does that have to do with ghosts?"

"It's the way our minds work," Ian explained. "You watch a scary movie and suddenly your home is filled with creaks and noises you never heard before. Were they always there? Of course they were. But you didn't pay attention because you weren't making connections."

"But after a day or so, the scary movie sounds go away," Mary said.

"Because that connection was short-lived and you can convince yourself in a day or so that it was merely a movie, not real life, and so you replace it with other connections," he said. "Bradley will be mooning over peanut butter for years…"

Mary smiled, reached over and grasped Bradley's hand. "I certainly hope so."

He lifted her hand to his mouth and kissed it. "I can guarantee it."

"And now, because of the work they've been doing with you, Rosie and Stanley are making connections," Ian continued. "They are looking for the quick movements out of the corner of their eyes, instead of ignoring them. They are listening for the whispers in the dark. They are paying attention to the movement of the doors. They are suddenly aware of the world of the dead, and I believe the dead are becoming bolder because they realize it too."

"Are bolder ghosts more dangerous?" Bradley asked.

"It just depends on their relationship with the person they're haunting," Ian said. "If they only want to warn them or send them a message, a bolder ghost is more helpful because the message will come through clearly. But if they are malevolent and they mean someone harm, well then, it's not so good."

"I think Rosie's ghost should be the first priority," Bradley said. "And maybe a couple of us spend the night there."

"Aye, I'd like to see the look on the ghost's face when he cuddles up in bed and finds one of us in there instead of Rosie," Ian agreed.

Chuckling, Bradley agreed. "It should be an interesting experience for all of us."

Chapter Seventeen

For the next two hours the conversation about ghosts was replaced with developing a plan to find Clarissa.

"I've sent Sean a copy of the photo we picked up at their home," Bradley explained, as they took the Sycamore exit. "He's going to work with Social Services and see what he can do. He mentioned that we ought to speak with Bernie."

"Bernie Wojchichowski?" Mary asked, alarmed that her brother mentioned the Chicago Coroner. "Does he think she might be dead?"

Shaking his head, Bradley explained. "No, Sean said that Bernie's daughter, Zoe, does some investigative work in the city," he said. "And she's got some unusual contacts that might be able to help us."

"I'm thinking Becca has run as far underground as she can," Ian said. "Especially if she thought Gary had money and the law on his side."

"So, we've gone through a list of all of the services she might use, we've developed a history of the schools Becca went to as a girl, the neighborhood she grew up in and any other contacts she might have made before they left Chicago," Mary said, as she read through her pages of notes. "And we know that she needs her prescription from somewhere and might be able to track her with that information."

"But we also know that she's very smart," Bradley said. "And quite paranoid and will avoid anything that a private investigator might use to track them down."

Mary sighed. "We are literally searching for someone who is doing everything not to be found."

"Aye," Ian agreed. "But we'll find her."

Bradley nodded. "Yes we will."

A few minutes later they pulled up next to the DeKalb County Courthouse. The large white stone building with its four massive pillars adjacent to the front entrance was an imposing structure with over one hundred years of judicial history.

"There's already a crowd of reporters on the front steps," Mary noted, as they skirted the front of the building. "Do you know any back ways in?"

Bradley guided the cruiser to the side of the building and parked in a lot filled with Sheriff Department vehicles. "One of the perks of being an officer of the law," he said. "All we have to do is go in this side door and we should be home free."

Bradley led them through a door on the side guarded by a county deputy. With a nod to Bradley, once Bradley had shown him his identification, they entered the building and walked to the large oak double doors that led to the courtroom.

Mary stopped in front of the doors and took a deep breath.

"How are you doing?" Bradley asked Mary.

She nodded, but bit her lower lip. Once inside those doors she knew she'd see him again. She closed her eyes and forced herself to breath calmly, but she could already feel her skin crawl as she recalled his hands on her, his voice taunting her and the total helplessness she had felt as his prisoner.

"You are not Jeannine," Ian whispered into her ear. "You are Mary O'Reilly and you can kick his arse."

Mary smiled and turned to Ian. "Thank you," she took another deep breath and finally met Bradley's eyes. "I'm good. I'll be fine."

"Of course she'll be fine, she's an O'Reilly," Sean said as he approached the group.

"Sean," Mary said, throwing her arms around her brother. "It's good to see you."

"Well, I had to be here to watch my little sister testify," he said with a wink. "Besides, they have me on the docket to testify today too."

"Why are you testifying?" Bradley asked.

Sean shrugged. "Because I was part of the investigative team, I suppose."

He turned to Ian. "How about you? Are you taking a turn on the stand?"

"Aye, but only as a witness to Mary's kidnapping," he said. "The other information is...not quite standard testimony."

"Yeah, they'd carry you off to a padded room if you start telling them about ghosts," he agreed. "But that's okay; we have him on this one. There's no way he's going to walk."

110

They entered the courtroom and walked toward the bench behind the prosecutor's table. Bradley and Sean flanked Mary on either side, and Ian walked behind her. As they approached the front of the courtroom, a door near the judge's table opened and Gary Copper entered the room. He was restrained in handcuffs and wore a bright orange jumpsuit. Two burly deputies escorted him toward the defense table.

As he scanned the room, his eyes came to rest on Mary. His face widened into a leering smile. "Why Mary, you're looking lovely today," he said, his eyes slowly taking in every inch of her body. "I've thought about you as I've sat in my cell. I thought about you a lot."

A frisson of terror rushed through her and although she wanted to run, she couldn't move.

"Tell me you missed me too," he purred and then he pursed his lips and mocked a kiss.

Mary's stomach clenched and she felt light-headed, but she wasn't going to let him win. "I didn't think of you once," she said, trying to appear unaffected.

He smiled at her again and met her eyes. "Don't worry, Mary, next time we're together it will be unforgettable. I promise."

She gasped and felt the bile rise in her throat. Bradley stepped in front of Mary and glared at the deputies. "Get him away from here, now," he ordered.

The deputies pulled him over to the table and locked his handcuffs to the bolt under the tabletop so his motions were limited. Sean put his arm around Mary's shoulders and guided her to the bench.

"Good girl," he whispered. "You didn't let him get to you."

"I feel like I'm going to throw up," she whispered.

"Well, don't do it now," he said. "I'm wearing my best suit."

She looked up at him in disbelief. "I'm going to be sick and you're worried about your suit?" she asked.

"Well, I've got to wear it this weekend to Rosie and Stanley's wedding," he explained. "And if it smells bad, I'm going to tell them it's your fault."

"You are an idiot," she whispered.

"But you love me anyway," Sean said, and then he put his thumb under her chin and lifted her head so he could look into her face. "Better?"

She took a deep breath and nodded. "Yeah, I am, thanks," she said.

Ian slipped in next to Sean and leaned around him to see Mary. "How're you doing, darling?" he asked.

She smiled weakly at him. "Good," she said, taking a deep breath. "I'm not going to let him get to me."

"You're quite a warrior," he replied. "There's got to be some Scottish in you somewhere."

112

That comment earned him a growl from Sean and a grin from Mary.

"Don't be jealous, Sean, me boy," Ian said. "I'm sure if Mary has some Scottish, so do you."

After conferring with the deputies, Bradley came around the other side of the bench and sat next to Mary, taking both of her hands in his. "You don't have to do this," he whispered. "We can walk out right now."

She looked up into his eyes, and then over to Ian and Sean, and felt her body relax. *I'm such an idiot,* she thought. *Not only am I stronger than Gary Copper ever was, but I have a group of men who would never let him get near me again. What in the world am I worried about?*

She exhaled softly, smiled at the men hovering over her and then laughed out loud, releasing the rest of her tension. She stood up and looked around. The judge and the attorneys were not yet in the room. She didn't want to do anything that would jeopardize the case, but she needed to wipe the smirk from Copper's face.

Standing, she scooted past Bradley. He caught her hand and looked at her with a question in his eye. "Don't worry," she said, nodding with total assurance. "I've got this one covered."

Walking over to the deputies, she extended her hand. "Hi, I'm Mary O'Reilly," she said.

"Yeah, Ms. O'Reilly, we heard about you," one of the large men said. "What can we do to help you?"

She glanced beyond them to Gary, sitting smugly in his seat. "I just want to respond to his last comment," she said. "That's all. Is that alright?"

"Well, ma'am, it's fine with us," he replied. "But you don't need to put yourself out."

She smiled at him. "Oh, no, it's something I really need to do."

She approached Gary and this time it was her turn to look him over, studying him like he was an insect on the floor. Then she placed her hands on the edge of the table and leaned toward him. "Perhaps you forgot how I kicked your ass the last time we met," she said. "And that was when I was drugged and weak. If there is a next time for us to meet, it will be unforgettable, because I won't be holding back and you won't be intimidating anyone."

His eyes widened for a moment and then tightened as he glared at her. "Bitch," he whispered angrily. "You don't scare me."

"Then you are a very stupid man," she stated unemotionally.

She met his eyes for one more moment, she was resolute and unafraid. Then she turned and walked away from him.

Chapter Eighteen

Clarissa hurried down the tall black steps of the CTA bus and turned and waved to her mother through the window. The doors closed with a whoosh of compressed air and the bus pulled away from the curb next to Clarissa's school, carrying her mother on to the restaurant where she worked. Even though the daily cost of a bus ride caused their budget to be even tighter, the two mile walk from the apartment building to the school was more than her mother could handle, especially when the weather was below freezing.

Clarissa readjusted her backpack and waited for the light to turn green, so she could cross over to the front of the school. She had barely stepped off the curb when she was joined by a group of older boys from the school. She had seen one of the boys hanging around in front of her apartment building, talking with her babysitter, Mrs. Gunderson.

"Hey, ain't you Clarissa?" he asked, as the rest of the boys circled her. "I seen you talking with my auntie."

She nodded. "Yes, I'm Clarissa," she replied.

"You love your momma?" he asked, and the other boys laughed and slapped him on his back.

She nodded and fear began to creep into her heart.

The boy smiled, but the smile wasn't in his eyes, it was a mean smile. "Well, that's good, 'cause you don't want your momma to die, do you?"

Shaking her head fervently, she tried not to cry. "I don't want my mother to die," she whispered.

They stopped her on the other side of the street, before she was able to enter the tall iron fence of the school yard. "Then you just gotta do what you're told," he said. "You got money in your backpack?"

She started to shake her head.

"You lie to me, girl, and your momma dies."

She thought of the envelope with the crisp dollar bills her mother had carefully counted out that morning. The money to pay for the babysitter. She slowly nodded to the boy. "I have money, but it's s'posed to go to Mrs. Gunderson," she said. "It's not my money. I don't have money. It's your aunt's money."

"That bitch don't need this money," he said. "I do. And you need to give it to me so your momma don't dic one of these nights when she comes home from work."

She looked into his face and knew he wasn't lying. She had seen the fights in the alleyways next to the school. She had seen the knives carefully hidden in backpacks. She had heard about classmates who no longer came to school because they had been killed in drive-by shootings, had heard Mrs. Gunderson talking about the murders in their neighborhood. She had no doubt the boys would do exactly what they said.

Reaching inside the zippered pocket of her backpack, she grasped the envelope. "Don't kill my mother," she said, her hand shaking as she held out the money.

He grabbed it from her and stuffed it into his pocket. "You just saved your momma's life," he said. "But if you tell anyone about this, even your momma, I'll find you and I'll kill both you and your momma. You understand?"

Clarissa nodded.

"Now, you best go to school little girl," the boy laughed. "And I'll be back next month for your next payment."

Clarissa ran down the street, away from the boys mocking laughter. Her heart was pounding and she felt like she was going to be sick. When she walked into the schoolyard a teacher approached her. "Are you okay, Clarissa?" the kindly teacher asked. "Did those boys bother you?"

Clarissa took a deep breath and did something that was becoming easier and easier every day. She lied to her teacher. "Oh, no, Mrs. Jankiewicz," she said. "They just live in the same apartment building as I do. I know their aunt."

Mrs. Jankiewicz looked over at the boys and then back at Clarissa. "Are you sure there isn't something you'd like to tell me?" she asked. "I promise you won't get in trouble."

Clarissa shook her head, her heart beating wildly. Would they think she had spoken with the teacher? Would they hurt her mother?

"No, but thank you Mrs. Jankiewicz," she replied firmly, taking a step away.

"But Clarissa…" the teacher insisted.

"Sorry, I have to go," Clarissa interrupted and walked away from the teacher. When she was halfway across the schoolyard, she glanced back at the boys. They were still watching her. Mrs. Gunderson's nephew nodded his head slightly and she let out a shuddering breath. Her mother was still safe. She walked past the playground equipment and sat by herself on a bench near the school. She wrapped her arms around her body and shivered from the cold as well as the fear growing in her stomach. She would have to be sure her mother never realized the babysitting money had been taken. No one could find out.

She looked up into the cold blue sky and watched as one fluffy white cloud floated by. It was long and narrow and looked like an angel. She sighed deeply. "I miss you, Daddy," she whispered, wiping a solitary tear from her eye. "I miss you lots."

Chapter Nineteen

Rosie came down the stairs at Mary's house a full two hours after Mary and Ian had left, rubbing the sleep from her eyes. "Morning, Rosie," Stanley offered cautiously from the kitchen table. "How'd you sleep last night?"

She yawned and stretched. "Oh, I had an awful sleep," she admitted. "The snoring from downstairs was just awful. It shook the house."

Stanley stood and pulled out a chair for her. "Don't I know it," he said. "I don't know how a man that young can have breathing issues like that. Must be all that time spent in drafty castles."

Rosie sat down and poured herself a cup of tea.

"Muffin?" Stanley offered, reaching inside the covered bowl for a blueberry muffin.

"Thank you," Rosie replied, biting into the crumbly pastry. "You know, these aren't bad. Mary did a fine job with these."

Stanley took a bite out of his second muffin and grumbled. "They's fine, but they ain't nothing compared to what you can whip up in the kitchen," he said.

She smiled sweetly. "Why thank you Stanley."

Looking away from her, Stanley perused the ceiling for a few moments before he cleared his throat and turned back her way. "Rosie."

"Yes, Stanley."

"I s'pose I need to apologize for how I acted last night."

"How's that?" she asked.

"Pretty much acted like an ass," he admitted.

She took another bite of muffin and nodded. "Why yes, I believe you did."

"Well you don't have to agree with me," he grumbled.

She hid her grin and nodded. "Of course, how rude of me," she said. "No, Stanley, you were just fine last night."

"But I acted like an ass," he said. "There ain't no two ways around it."

She sighed. "What would you like me to say?"

He pushed back his chair and stood up. "I don't know," he growled. "I want to be the one you run to, Rosie."

Placing his hands on the edge of the table, he leaned over toward her. "I want to be the one to protect you. Guess I was just plain jealous that you came here."

"But, Stanley, I was only looking for a place to spend the night," she said. "I would have come to you to solve my problem with the ghost in the morning."

"Really?" he asked. "You weren't coming here so they could fight your battles?"

Shaking her head, she reached over and placed her hand over his. "Stanley, you're my hero," she replied. "There's no one I would run to for help before you."

He leaned over further and kissed her forehead. "You humble me, Rosie."

"I do no such thing, Stanley," she said, reaching up and kissing him back. "I just want to be sure we understand each other."

He smiled at her. "Well, I ain't saying I understand woman, and I ain't saying I don't," he said. "But I know it's gonna be fun figuring each other out."

"Yes, it is, Stanley. Yes it is."

They sat in companionable silence for a few moments until Rosie delicately cleared her throat. "Um, Stanley," she began.

He looked up from the newspaper he was reading. "Yes?"

"Did I hear you correctly last night when you mentioned that you were being haunted by your first wife, Verna?"

He nodded. "As best as I could see it was her," he said. "But it weren't her, if you know what I mean."

Rosie stirred her tea, began to lift it to her mouth, but then placed it down on the table. "Do you still love her?" she finally asked. "Is that the reason she's haunting you? Are you regretting your decision to ask me to marry you?"

Stanley dropped the paper and sat back in his chair, shocked. "Where in tarnation did that idea come from?" he asked. "I ain't haunting her, she's haunting me. I didn't ask her to come walking through my bedroom, rustling through my drawers. She just took it upon herself."

Putting her hands on the edge of the table, Rosie leaned toward him. "You didn't answer my question, Stanley Aloysius Wagner," she demanded. "Do you still love Verna?"

He reached over and took her hand, and although she tried to resist, he held it firmly. "Look at me, Rosie," he said softly, and waited until she met his eyes. "Of course I still love Verna. She was my first wife. We grew up together, we worked together, we had kids together and we lived a whole lot of years together. Just 'cause someone dies doesn't mean the love dies too."

"But what about me?" Rosie asked quietly.

"Love ain't a pie, Rosie," he explained. "You don't only got so much to go around. Loving someone don't take the love from someone else. I love Verna, but it's an old love, soft and sweet, filled with memories of years gone by. I love you, but it's a burning love. It's new and fresh and kinda exciting. It's a different love than the one I had with Verna because you're a different woman. Does that make sense to you?"

"Why Stanley I think that's the most talking you've done since I've met you," Rosie replied with a smile. "It does make sense to me. Thank you for being honest with me."

He lifted her hand and brought it to his lips for a quick kiss. "I may not be too romantical, and I may not say all the right things," he said. "But I do promise that I will be honest with you."

"And that's the best promise of all," she replied. "Besides, who says you're not romantic? I think you are the most romantic man I've ever met. I don't blame Verna for coming back."

He shook his head. "That's the strangest thing," he said. "I can't understand why after all these years she'd even want to come back."

"Did she say anything to you?"

He thought for a moment. "She told me to don't forget."

"Don't forget what?"

"Don't know," he said. "I s'pose I forgot."

"Well, maybe I can help you remember," Rosie suggested. "Let's go back to your place and see if we can find what she was looking for."

Stanley hesitated. "You sure you want to do that?" he asked.

Rosie stood up, picked up her tea cup and placed it in the sink. "Of course I do," she said. "Besides, it's past time I met Verna."

Rolling his eyes, Stanley stood too. "No good's gonna come from this," he muttered to himself. "I can feel it in my bones."

Chapter Twenty

"Bernard…Woja…Watcha…Woji…" the court reporter stumbled over the name.

"Wojchichowski, ma'am," Bernie offered, as he lumbered up the steps to the witness stand. "Bernard Wojchichowski. But most folks call me Bernie, it's easier."

A fleeting smile quickly slipped from her face and she faced Bernie. "Bernie, then," she began. "Please put your right hand on the Bible. Do you swear to tell the truth, the whole truth and nothing but the truth, so help you God?"

Bernie nodded solemnly. "Yes, ma'am, I do."

"Please be seated."

Bernie sat on the chair and looked out over the courtroom. It was packed with reporters and people from the community eager to learn more about the salacious crimes perpetrated by the formerly well-respected dentist.

The attorney for the prosecution, Lydia Meyers, a thin middle-aged woman, came forward. "Can you tell the jury what your occupation is?" she asked.

"I'm the Cook County Coroner," Bernie replied.

"And what is your main duty in this job?"

"My main job is to determine the cause of death, when it happened and how it happened," he replied.

"Did you, in your duties as coroner, review the remains of Jeannine Alden?" Lydia asked.

Bernie nodded. "Yeah, I reviewed what was left of them after Copper hid them in a grave under someone else's name," he replied.

"Objection," Greg Thanner, the defense attorney, a morbidly obese middle-aged man, cried. "Answer exceeds scope of question and constitutes a volunteered statement by the witness."

"Hey, I got no problem volunteering information," Bernie said with a shrug. "So the jury can get any information you forget to ask me about."

Mary leaned over toward Bradley. "Go Bernie," she whispered.

"Sustained," the judge called out, rapping her gavel sharply. "The witness will not volunteer any extraneous information."

Bernie turned to the judge. "Does that mean I can't give out extra information?"

The judge nodded. "Indeed it does," she replied.

"Mr. Wojchichowski, what was the cause of death of Jeannine Alden?" Lydia asked.

"I was unable to determine cause of death from the remains," Bernie testified, folding his arms over his chest and sitting back in the chair.

"But the death certificate I have in my hand states she died of a heart attack," she stated.

Bernie nodded.

The attorney looked confused.

"If you could not determine the cause of death through her remains, why did you put heart attack on the death certificate?"

Bernie leaned forward in his chair and met the attorney's eyes. "Because she died of a heart attack," Bernie replied simply.

"And you know this because…?" the attorney prompted.

Bernie turned in his chair and looked up at the judge. "Is it okay with you that I give her more information?"

The judge rolled her eyes and nodded while several members of the jury chuckled. Bernie turned and winked at them.

The judge rapped her gavel again. "The witness will answer the question."

"I know this because once it was determined that this was the body of Jeannine Alden and not Beverly Copper, as was listed on the gravestone as well as the death certificate," he began, "I called the hospital to confirm the cause of death. Jeannine Alden died of a drug-induced heart attack because the hospital was looking at the medical records of Beverly Copper and did not know of Jeannine Alden's allergy to the drug they gave her after delivery."

"So due to information that was falsified on her entrance to the hospital, Jeannine Alden died," the attorney concluded.

Bernie nodded his head. "That's the way I see it," he said. "If Copper hadn't lied about Jeannine being his wife, she'd still be with us today."

"Thank you, Mr. Wojchichowski. No further questions, your honor," she said, walking back to her chair.

"Would the defense like to cross-examine the witness?" the judge asked.

Mopping his brow with a soiled handkerchief, Greg stood up slowly and lumbered forward. "We would, your honor," he said.

Templing his fingertips on his large protruding belly, he approached Bernie. "Did Dr. Copper administer the drug that killed Jeannine Alden?" the defense attorney asked.

"No, but..." Bernie began.

"Was there any proof that Dr. Copper knew Ms. Alden was allergic to that specific drug?" he asked.

"Well, no," he said. "But..."

"That's all I have your honor," the attorney interrupted, and then he turned to Bernie. "You may step down."

"But..." Bernie tried again.

"You may step down," the judge ordered.

Bernie glared at the attorney, but stepped down as he was asked and made his way back to his seat several rows behind Mary and Bradley.

Mary turned around and sent him an encouraging smile, but Bernie did not seem satisfied with his testimony.

"The prosecution would like to call Doctor Rachael Drummond to the stand," the court reporter called.

A tall, nicely dressed African American woman walked forward. Mary recognized her as the doctor who had helped with Jeannine's delivery. The woman stepped forward, took the oath and then sat down in front of the attorney.

"Can you repeat your name?" Lydia asked.

"Dr. Rachael Drummond," she replied.

"And where do you work?"

"Cook County Hospital," she replied.

"How many years have you worked at Cook County?" he asked.

"For nearly fifteen years," she replied.

"What department do you work in?"

"I work in Labor and Delivery," she replied. "I've worked in that area for over ten years."

The attorney picked up a photo of Jeannine and showed it to the doctor. "Do you recognize this woman?" she asked.

The doctor studied the photo and nodded. "Yes, I see a lot of patients," she admitted. "But this woman's face will haunt me for the rest of my life."

"Her name was Jeannine Alden," Lydia supplied.

The doctor shook her head. "I thought her name was Beverly."

"So you recall she died on the table about eight years ago after giving birth to a baby girl because you administered Syntometrine to her and she had an allergic reaction," she stated baldly.

Dr. Drummond nodded mutely and took a moment to compose herself. "Yes, of course I remember her," she said, her voice emotional. "She came in late one evening, in the late fall. She was under the influence of something and was barely coherent. We helped her through labor and when she started bleeding we gave her a shot of Syntometrine. She reacted badly immediately."

"Was there a hospital investigation regarding the death?" she asked.

The doctor nodded. "Yes, of course, there was," she said. "Her patient form, which was filled out by her husband, did not include her allergy. We were acting in the patient's best interest when we administered the drug. And, due to her inebriated state, she was unable to clearly communicate with us that she was allergic to the drug. The hospital was found faultless in the investigation."

Lydia crossed back to her table and then turned to face the doctor. "Did you do an autopsy of the woman to determine what caused her inebriation?" Lydia asked.

She nodded. "Yes, when a patient dies at the hospital, we require an autopsy."

"And what drugs were indicated?" Lydia asked, moving forward.

"It was just as Dr. Copper thought," Rachael said. "She had taken Valium."

"Dr. Copper suggested that she had taken the drug?"

"Yes," Rachael said. "When he rushed her in through the ER he said that she had gotten into his Valium."

"Did you see any evidence that this was a reoccurring problem?" Lydia asked.

The doctor shook her head. "Valium is one of the drugs that is hard to trace," she said. "It leaves the system quickly and leaves no trace evidence. It was only because she still had it in her system that we were able to classify it."

Lydia moved to the side of the witness stand. "Do you see her husband in this courtroom?" the attorney asked.

The doctor looked around the room and zeroed in on Gary Copper. "There he is," she said and pointed to him.

"So, this man, Gary Copper, told you that this woman, Jeannine Alden, was his wife?" she asked.

The doctor nodded.

"Do you remember specifically him referring to her as his wife?" Lydia asked.

"Yes, we were rushing her in and he kept yelling that his wife was in labor and we needed to help her."

"And on the hospital form, he put her name down as Beverly Copper?" Lydia asked.

"Yes, and that was the name I put on the death certificate," she added.

"In your professional opinion, do you find that most husbands are aware of the drugs their wives are allergic to?" Lydia questioned.

"Well, when it's a drug that can cause death, yes," the doctor said.

"Objection," Greg called, "opinion. I doubt if the good doctor has actually done a study on the information offered by spouses to determine the percentage of accuracy."

"I did ask for her opinion, your honor," Lydia reiterated. "I did not ask for statistics or evidentiary information."

"Overruled," the judge agreed. "You may continue with your questioning."

"Actually, I've completed my questions for the witness, your honor," Lydia said.

"Mr. Thanner, your witness," the judge indicated.

Greg stood, scraping his chair against the wood floor of the courtroom. He flipped through a manila file for a moment and then made his way around the desk to the front of the witness station. "Dr. Drummond, did Dr. Copper in any way suggest that you give her the Syntometrine?" he asked.

The doctor shook her head. "No, of course not," she said. "He wasn't even in the labor room with us."

"So, he was not even in the same room with you when Jeannine Alden died? Wasn't even aware of the procedure you were going to perform on her?" the attorney asked pointedly.

"No, because of the risk involved with her delivery, we had him wait outside," she said.

"No further questions," the attorney said. "You may step down."

Chapter Twenty-one

Several hours later, after a number of witnesses testified, including Jeannine's parents, Bradley and Jeannine's neighbors and co-workers, the court called a recess. Mary, Bradley, Sean and Ian found an antechamber where they could talk away from the interrogation of the news reporters.

"I'll be back in a minute," Sean said. "I want to see if I can pull Bernie in here."

Sean closed the door behind him and made his way quickly through the crowd. Bernie was next to the staircase plugging some quarters into the pop machine. Sean came up behind him. "I hear that stuff is like embalming fluid to your insides," he said.

The vending machine whirred and the can tumbled down to the opening. Bernie picked it up, popped back the tab and took a large gulp. "Yeah, don't I know it," he said with a smile. "But I think of it this way; it saves a lot of time in the end."

Sean grinned. "You did good on the stand," he said, patting the large man's arm. "Real good."

"You know why I never became a lawyer?" Bernie asked.

"Because you weren't smart enough?" Sean responded with a grin.

Bernie chuckled. "No, because I like to uncover all the truth, not just the pieces I want the jury to see," he said. "That defense attorney's not doing an autopsy; he's not even shaving all the hair off the body. He's just slapping make-up on a corpse and calling it a day."

Sean nodded. "He's doing his job, whether we like it or not."

"I felt like a trained monkey in there," Bernie grumbled, taking another sip of cola. "It's not a feeling I like."

Sean looked up and saw several members of the media making their way toward them. "Hey, Bernie, we got a nice quiet room down the hall, away from the news hounds," he said. "Why don't you come on down? I know that Mary wanted to talk to you."

Bernie nodded. "Yeah, sure, that'd be great," he said. "It'll keep me from putting my foot in my mouth."

Sean grinned and guided him back into the room.

"It's like a feeding frenzy out there," Bernie said as they closed the door. "How are you guys holding up?"

"Ah, well, just fine, if you don't mind watching a fairy tale come alive before you," Ian complained. "By the end of the day, they'll be giving the man a medal instead of locking him in the deep, dark place he belongs."

Bernie shrugged. "I did the best I could do. I know it wasn't..."

Ian put his hand on Bernie's shoulder. "You did a great job," he said. "You got in more information than anyone else has been allowed to. You gave that lawyer a run for his money and we're all grateful to you. It just burns me to see the way he's being portrayed."

"Well, don't worry," Sean said. "Once Bradley takes the stand, things will get cleared up."

There was a quick knock on the door and Sean opened it to see the bailiff standing outside. "Court's about to resume," he said. "We need you to take your seats."

Mary grasped Bradley's hand quickly, squeezed it and then let it go. "For luck," she said.

"Thanks, I think I'm going to need it," he replied.

Once inside the courtroom, Bradley was called to the stand and sworn in. He sat tall in the chair and looked slowly around the courtroom. He looked at the jury, their eyes focused on the attorney. Bradley could see the attorney had them captivated with his version of the story. Then he looked over at Gary, who sat calm and relaxed in his chair. Gary met Bradley's eyes and nodded his head slightly and smirked at him.

He knows he's winning, Bradley thought, his blood boiling. *Well, I'm not going to let that bastard get away with killing my wife.*

Lydia approached Bradley. "Chief Alden, how do you know Dr. Gary Copper?"

"He was a neighbor of mine in Sycamore," Bradley answered. "And he is the man who kidnapped and killed my wife."

Members of the jury inhaled sharply, but the attorney did not object.

"Chief Alden, weren't you in fact more than just neighbors with Dr. Copper?" he asked. "Didn't you consider him a close friend of both yourself and your wife?"

"A trusted friend," he admitted. "He and his wife, Beverly, were invited to our home many times."

"Could you please tell us what happened at your home eight years ago?"

"I was on patrol," he explained. "I was an officer for the Sycamore Police Department. And we received a call about a home invasion. Then the dispatcher gave us the address and I realized it was my home. I rushed to the scene and found my house had been broken into, our possessions scattered and my wife was missing."

"How did you react?" Lydia asked.

"I beg your pardon, but how do you think I reacted?" he said. "My wife was pregnant. We had just found out we were having a baby girl. Just purchased the pink paint for the nursery. I was frantic. I searched through the house again, even though other officers had done the same."

"When did you stop searching?" Lydia asked.

"I searched for seven years," he said. "Gave up my job, my pension, my savings in order to find my wife. I followed every lead I could, searched

136

morgues for Jane Does, and did everything I could. Until I realized I had no more leads and had done all I could. That's when I took the job in Freeport, as police chief."

"What led you to the discovery of Gary Copper's relationship with your wife?"

"I hired a private investigator and she discovered that Gary drugged Jeannine with Valium and kept her in a subterranean room, underneath his office, until she was in labor. Then, in a panic, he brought her to Cook County Hospital, so no one would know who he was. When she died, he buried her using his wife's name."

"Wouldn't his wife object to that?"

"She probably would have if he didn't have his wife and their baby stuffed into the freezer in his basement at his home," Bradley stated.

The jury and the courtroom audience gasped.

"Objection," Greg called. "Inadmissible evidence."

"I was there! I saw the bodies!" Bradley countered, leaning forward on the stand.

Greg ignored Bradley and spoke directly to the judge. "Chief Alden entered the home without a warrant and with no probable cause that a crime was being committed."

"There was probable cause," Lydia argued. "Mary O'Reilly had been kidnapped by Copper, the same way he took Jeannine."

Lumbering up from his seat, Greg leaned forward on his desk. "And what proof do you have that Dr. Copper did that, Ms. Meyer?" he asked. "None that you've presented to the bench."

"The police found Ms. O'Reilly at Dr. Copper's office after she had been forcibly removed from her home," Lydia countered.

"My client told me that Ms. O'Reilly seduced him and coerced him to take her back to his office," Greg said with a mocking sneer. "Something about always wanting to do it in a dentist chair."

"What the hell!" Bradley shouted, standing up in his chair and lunging toward Greg. The big man jumped back and knocked his chair over.

"Order!" the judge shouted, as she rapped her gavel sharply on the desk. "Order in this court!"

Bradley sat down slowly, his glare never leaving Greg's face. Mopping his forehead again, Greg took a deep shaky breath. "Permission to approach the bench," he stammered.

Nodding, the judge motioned to Lydia. "I think it would be a good idea for both of you to approach."

When the lawyers stood in front of the judge she glared at Greg. "If I ever hear about you goading a witness as you just did with Chief Alden, I will have you disbarred. Do you understand me?"

Greg nodded. "Yes, your honor."

Then she turned to Lydia. "Do you have any evidence that Gary Copper kidnapped and kept Jeannine Alden against her will?"

"We have DNA evidence that she was down there," Lydia said. "But because she died, we only have circumstantial evidence."

"So, Chief Alden acted on circumstantial evidence and did not obtain a warrant before entering Dr. Copper's home," she summarized.

Lydia paused and then sighed. "Yes, your honor."

"Counselor, you are going to have to do a lot better than that if you are going to win your case," she stated. "Now, let's proceed."

Greg returned to his seat and Lydia walked back over to Bradley. She shook her head and whispered, "I'm sorry."

"The jury will disregard the information stated by the witness in regards to the contents of Dr. Copper's residence. A warrant was not obtained and therefore any evidence is inadmissible to this court."

"Chief Alden, when did you discover Dr. Copper had buried your wife using the name Beverly Copper?" she asked.

"A month ago we obtained a court order to have the body exhumed," he said. "The Cook County Coroner was able to perform a DNA test and confirm she was indeed Jeannine Alden, my wife."

"How long had your wife been dead?" she asked.

Bradley started to speak, but his voice cracked and he stopped and cleared his throat. "She was buried five months after the break-in," he said. "I searched for her for years, not knowing she was already dead and resting in a cemetery in Cook County. I searched for her, not knowing that our baby girl had been given up for adoption."

"Thank you, Chief Alden, no more questions."

"Mr. Thanner, would you like to cross-examine?"

Greg stood up. "Yes, your honor, I would," he said.

Staying safely behind his desk, Greg addressed Bradley. "Dr. Copper was your trusted friend for years, was he not?"

Bradley nodded tightly. "That was before I found out he was a psychopath."

"Chief Alden, do you have any psychological training that would allow you to classify anyone, including my client, as a psychopath?" he asked.

Bradley shook his head. "No official training, just years on the police force," he replied.

The attorney smiled and nodded. He reached forward and picked up a manila folder. "Ah, yes, your years on the force," he repeated, holding the folder in one hand and waving it toward Bradley. "It's funny you should mention that."

He walked slowly up to the stand. "According to your personnel records, in fact, you were the person who was deemed mentally unstable," the attorney said. "Let me read the exact words the police psychologist used in your fitness for duty evaluation: 'Officer Alden has become psychologically impaired and it is our recommendation that he be restricted to desk duty. His behavior is obsessive, aggressive and compulsive. He is also showing minor signs of paranoia in regards to the work of his fellow officers.'"

The attorney looked up at Bradley. "Do you recall this evaluation?" he asked.

"It was given to me approximately twelve months after the disappearance of my wife," he said. "I had been searching for her on my off hours."

The attorney nodded. "Yes, the disappearance of your wife," he said. "You stated that you were on duty that day and received a call of a break in. Is that correct?"

Bradley nodded. "Yes."

"And you got to your home to find the house ransacked and your wife missing. Is that correct?"

"Yes, that's correct."

"Your police chief held you back. He kept you from entering your home. Correct?"

"That's normal police procedure when the officer is personally connected to the crime," Bradley explained.

"Yes, normal police procedure," the attorney reiterated. "And is it normal police procedure for your captain to ask you if your wife could have staged the break-in in order to escape from an unhappy marriage?"

"We were not unhappy," Bradley shouted. "We were happy. We were going to have a baby."

The attorney picked up another folder. "If your wife was so happy, why did she seek the counsel of a divorce lawyer a year before the break in?" he asked.

Bradley took a deep breath. "We had some problems; work, scheduling, communication," he said to the jury. "But after we saw Gary and Beverly's marriage collapse, we decided we both needed to work harder on our relationship. When she disappeared we had no problems with our marriage. We were happy, thrilled that our baby was coming."

The attorney shrugged. "No problems that you were aware of, perhaps," he said. "But did it ever cross your mind, even once while you searched for your wife, that she might have staged her disappearance? Remember, Chief Alden, you are under oath."

Bradley paused for a moment, and then slowly nodded. "Yes, it did cross my mind," he said slowly. "But…"

"That's all I need to hear," the attorney interrupted.

"But…" Bradley began again.

"That's enough, Chief Alden," he repeated.

The attorney started sit down, then stopped and looked up. "Oh, one more thing, Chief Alden," he said. "While you were searching for your wife for nearly eight years, you ran into some financial issues with your house payments. You were going to lose your home. Who helped you save your home? Who lent you money with no strings attached?"

"Gary did," Bradley admitted.

"Gary did," the attorney repeated. "And you accepted that money because you believed him to be a trusted friend. Isn't that correct?"

"I did, before he kidnapped my wife," Bradley answered angrily.

"Isn't it possible, Chief Alden, that Jeannine felt he was a trusted friend too," the attorney asked, "and went to him for protection and security when she wanted to escape her marriage to you?"

"No!" he countered loudly. "She did not leave me for him. She was kidnapped. She was drugged and taken from our home."

The attorney turned fully and faced Bradley. "Once again, Chief Alden, do you have any evidence to back up these charges?" he asked, his eyebrow raised fractionally.

Bradley looked frantically at Mary and Ian and saw the frustration in their faces.

Nothing. I have nothing. The word of a ghost. Nothing to prove this in court.

"No, I have no evidence," he said slowly.

"No further questions, your honor," the attorney said.

"Chief Alden," the judge replied. "You may step down."

Chapter Twenty-two

Stanley unlocked his front door and cautiously pushed it open. Both he and Rosie peered around the door into the house and searched the room.

"What are we looking for?" Rosie whispered into his ear.

"Glowing lights," Stanley said over his shoulder, "in the hallway."

Rosie stood on her tiptoes to peer over Stanley's shoulder. "Isn't it hard to see glowing lights in the daytime?" she asked.

Stanley paused and then swung the door wide open. "Well, you didn't have to make it sound so obvious," he grumbled.

She bit back a laugh. "I'm sorry, Stanley," she said, stepping into the house behind him. "What would you suggest we do next?"

Putting his hands on his hips, he looked around the house. It hadn't been remodeled since Verna had died over fifteen years ago. The blond wooden bookcase and television stand still held the RCA Victor television set they had purchased the Christmas before she died. A shelf of VCR tapes sat next to the aging VCR player and the small DVD player his children had bought him for Christmas a few years back still sat in the box, unopened, next to it.

The cable box sat on top of the television, attached to the back by a series of connectors that modified the old hardware to communicate with the new. Even though it took the cable installer an hour to figure it out, Stanley told him he'd never have one of those new-fangled televisions that were thinner than a dinner plate in his home.

Pictures of his family hung on the wall over the television. From their wedding photo in black and white, to the last photo he and Verna took with their children, grandchildren and even a great-grandchild, they illustrated the history of his life.

He finally turned to Rosie, who stood waiting expectantly for his answer. "Guess I never stopped to really look at my house before," he said. "Guess it seems like I stopped moving forward when Verna died."

Rosie wrapped her arm around his waist and laid her head on his shoulder, looking at the photos in front of them. "You have a lovely family," she said. "And you should be proud of what you and Verna accomplished."

He slipped his arm around her waist, pulled her closer and pressed a kiss on her cheek. "Thank you."

Rosie stepped away and looked around the rest of the room. "Where did you say you saw her?" she asked.

Stanley walked through the living room of the small ranch-style home into the kitchen. "Well, the first time, I was here at the sink," he explained. "I was heating up some milk and helping myself to a piece of your strawberry rhubarb pie. I saw a glowing figure move from the office to the bedroom."

"Was your office disturbed?" she asked. "Did it look like she was searching in there?"

Looking a little embarrassed, Stanley hesitated.

"What?" Rosie asked.

Sighing, he held out his hand and, after taking hers, led her through the hall to the office. "As you can see," he explained, as he switched on the light, "I don't know if anybody could tell that someone was in here."

Gasping softly, Rosie looked around at the piles of papers, magazines, books and newspapers scattered around the room. "How do you ever find anything?" she asked.

"I got a system," Stanley grumbled. "Works just fine fer me."

Rosie turned and stared at him. "Stanley Wagner, you cannot tell me that Verna allowed you to have a room like this in her home," she said. "I just won't believe it."

Bending his head down, Stanley shuffled his foot for a moment. "Naw, she didn't," he confessed. "She would make me dig my space out regularly. Usually took me a couple of days to do it."

Shaking her head, Rosie turned and walked out of the room without saying a word. Stanley heard some rustling coming from the kitchen and in a moment Rosie was back with an empty garbage bag, a broom, a dust pan and a dust mop in her hands. "You have five days until we're married," she said, handing him the equipment. "You had better start cleaning now."

"But, but...what are you going to do?" he asked.

"I'll tidy your kitchen, I'll make your meals and I'll even try and organize the other rooms in your home," she said. "But you don't stop working on this room except to eat and sleep until it's clean."

"But how about television?" he asked. "The History Channel?"

She sent him a sideways look. "No television until the work is done," she declared. "And if you complain, I won't make any desserts."

"But, Ver...I mean Rosie," he began.

Placing her hands on her hips she stared at him for a moment. "And now I understand why she was haunting you," she said before turning and walking out of the room.

Chapter Twenty-three

A cold wind blew in the schoolyard and plastic grocery bags and newspapers were airborne as children dashed around them, making their way to the parked buses at the side of the schoolyard. Clarissa walked slowly through the playground. She knew that Mrs. Gunderson would be waiting in her car, an ancient Buick that spewed black smoke and smelled of old cigarettes and stale beer. But before the key was shoved into the ignition and the car coughed to life, Mrs. Gunderson would demand the envelope that contained her babysitting money. The envelope she no longer had.

If she told Mrs. Gunderson the truth, there was a good chance she would go after the boys for the money. One of the boys was her nephew, after all, the same nephew who promised with a smile that if she told anyone, her mother would be killed. A shiver went through Clarissa's body that had nothing to do with the cold. She knew, without a shadow of a doubt, those young men would kill her mother without a second thought.

If she didn't tell Mrs. Gunderson, she would find out soon enough, when the small zippered compartment was opened and no money was inside. She was pretty sure Mrs. Gunderson would throw her out of her car and leave her standing on the sidewalk in front of the school. She was also sure Mrs. Gunderson would accuse her of stealing the money or would accuse her mother of cheating her. Either way, her mother would find out the money was gone and that was one thing Clarissa couldn't let happen.

She paused at the corner of the school as an idea took hold in her mind. Bending down, she laid her backpack on the ground and picked up a sharp rock. She pounded on the zipper pull until the small metal tabs broke and then, for good measure, she pounded on the zipper slide until it was misshapen and couldn't be moved. With a small smile, she slipped the backpack on and skipped to the waiting car.

"What took you so long?" Mrs. Gunderson snapped. "I told you to come straight to me from your room. You hanging with some kids?"

Clarissa shook her head as she climbed into the car and tried to insert the rusted and filthy seatbelt into the buckle. "No, Mrs. Gunderson," she said. "The teacher had to help me with my backpack. Someone took it and broke it."

"What?!" she screamed. "My money's in that backpack. What the hell were you thinking?"

Clarissa shook her head. "The teacher said it looks like they tried to get into the pocket with your money, but they couldn't. She said we should take it home and use…" she paused, trying to remember the name of the tools her father used to use to open things. "Oh, yes, pliers…she said pliers would work to get it open."

Mrs. Gunderson grabbed the backpack and tried to force the zipper down, but it was stuck fast.

"Pliers? I ain't got no damn pliers in my apartment," Mrs. Gunderson complained, as she started the car. "Who does your teacher think I am, some damn plumber?"

Clarissa decided that was one of those questions she shouldn't answer.

Mrs. Gunderson maneuvered the large car around the block of the school and through a side street to the main boulevard. Clarissa looked over and watched the older woman's face. She could tell she was thinking about something because her mouth was moving, but no words were coming out. She did that a lot when she was thinking about things. Finally, she pasted a crooked smile on her face and turned to Clarissa. "So, sweetie, did anything unusual happen at school today?" she asked.

"I got an A on my spelling test," Clarissa responded innocently.

"I don't give a damn..." the woman caught herself. "I mean, that's good. That's great. But did anything happen on your way to school?"

She lifted her overly plucked eyebrows in encouragement and Clarissa thought she resembled a heron they had studied in school. "Well, let me see," Clarissa said slowly. "There was one thing."

"Yes, what happened Clarissa?"

"A lady on the bus smiled at me today," she responded with a bright smile.

150

"I mean after you got off the bus," she said tightly.

Clarissa could tell Mrs. Gunderson was ready to lose her temper and generally that meant she was going to get slapped again. She wondered why Mrs. Gunderson would ask her so many questions about what happened that morning. It was almost as if...

Mrs. Gunderson knew those boys were going to take the money! The thought burst into her mind with both speed and assurance. *Mrs. Gunderson wanted those boys to steal from me. She told them about the money. That's how they knew I was carrying it this morning.*

She turned a little on the seat and faced her babysitter. "Don't kill my mother, Mrs. Gunderson," she said softly. "Don't let them kill my mother."

Mrs. Gunderson sucked in her breath. "I don't know what you mean," she stammered. "What are you talking about?"

Clarissa took a deep breath. "You don't have to watch me anymore," she said. "I'll give them the money every month. But please, don't let them hurt my mother."

They arrived in front of the apartment complex and Mrs. Gunderson pulled the car to the curb. "I'm sure I don't know what you're talking about," she said, and then she leaned forward and met Clarissa's eyes. "And as long as you do what you're told, I'm sure your mother will be safe."

Clarissa met her eyes squarely; she didn't flinch or sink back. "That's fine," she said, "as long as you never tell my mother about this."

A cackle of laughter spilled from her mouth. "Tell her? Are you kidding me?" she spat. "This is the best deal I've had in a long time."

Clarissa nodded and reached for the door release. "Thank you," she said solemnly before she slipped out of the car and walked away.

Chapter Twenty-four

Mary opened the door to her house and immediately smelled the garlic and oregano of Italian cooking. Inhaling deeply, she realized suddenly that she was not only hungry, she was starving. "Rosie, I love you," she called from the doorway, as she pulled off her coat and hung it in the closet.

"Aye, I'll be seconding Mary on that," Ian said, dropping his coat on the couch and heading directly into the kitchen.

Apron-covered with two large spoons in her hands as she tossed a large salad, Rosie stood on the other side of the counter. "I thought you might be hungry after your day in court," she explained. "And I decided to give Stanley some time off for good behavior. Besides we were both dying to know what happened."

Ian lifted the edge of a red and white striped dish towel that was covering a large bowl and discovered large chunks of garlic bread. He picked out a piece, took a large bite and closed his eyes in satisfaction. "Thank you, Rosie," he said. "You have been the saving grace for an otherwise bloody frustrating day."

She looked past Ian to Mary. "Where's Bradley?" she asked. "What happened?"

"Bradley was returning some calls to his office," Mary explained. "He'll only be a few minutes. But Ian's right, things did not go well in court today."

Stanley walked over from the recliner, where he'd been watching television. "Seems like it ought to be an open and shut case," he said. "You let those lawyers twist your words?"

Ian glanced sharply at Stanley. "I wouldn't repeat that comment when Bradley's here," he said. "He took a beating on the stand and it wasn't his fault. How do you tell a judge and jury that you know your wife was kidnapped and repeatedly raped because her ghost told you about it?"

Stanley nodded. "Yeah, I could see the problem with that."

"They made it look like Jeannine ran away from Bradley and sought protection from Gary," Mary said. "They made it seem that Bradley was mentally unsound and Jeannine's only recourse was to hide from him."

Rosie slammed the wooden spoons down on the counter. "Why that's just ridiculous," she said. "Bradley is one of the best men I've ever met. He would never harm his wife; he's just too noble for that."

"Thank you, Rosie," Bradley said from the doorway. "Perhaps I need you to testify as a character witness."

He shrugged off his coat and hung it in the closet and joined the group in the kitchen. Mary met

154

him and gave him a hug. "You did a great job on the stand. You were able to bring out some issues that would have been hid from the jury otherwise."

"But they were overturned," he said with a shake of his head. "And we weren't able to use any information from his house. So the videos of his patients, the bodies in the freezer, nothing is admissible."

"Why not?" Stanley asked.

"Because I entered his house without a warrant," Bradley explained, gathering Mary in his arms. "Not that I would have done anything differently."

She laid her head on his chest. "Yes, I'm not sure if I would still be here if you waited around for a warrant."

"But you were able to mention them?" Rosie asked, pulling a stack of plates from Mary's cabinet.

Mary slipped out of Bradley's arms and took the plates from Rosie, walking over to the table and setting it.

"Doesn't matter," Ian said, walking over to the silverware drawer and pulling out forks and knives. "The jury's made up of humans. They can't erase information like that, as much as the judge would like them to. They might disregard the testimony, but that bit of information is going to color the way they look at Copper."

"Why the hell don't Mary just get up there and tell it like it is?" Stanley asked, strolling to the table and sitting down. "Surely in this day and age people understand we have more than our five senses to work with. Don't the government use psychics as spies?"

Ian leaned back against the counter and pulled out another slice of bread. "Well, it's said they used to use them during the Cold War," Ian said. "But the government has never confirmed that information. And, unfortunately, because there are so many charlatans out there who claim they have psychic ability, the entire group has been labeled as frauds."

"But you and Mary are the real thing," Rosie insisted. "Can't you demonstrate your skills in the courtroom?"

He took another bite of the bread. "Aye, we could have Jeannine testify in court through Mary and state something only she would know," he said. "But the problem with that is only Jeannine, and perhaps Gary, know it to be true. There's no way to prove what we're saying."

Bradley reached past Ian and took a piece of bread for himself. Biting it, he smiled at Rosie. "Thank you," he said. "I needed this. And to echo Ian's point, psychic testimony is inadmissible in court. So, even if Mary convinced the judge and jury, and I have no doubt she could do it, the law would not allow it and Gary could get a mistrial."

"Well, I guess my moment of truth comes tomorrow," Mary said, placing water cups next to the plates. "And after watching what happened today on the stand, I can tell you I'm not looking forward to it."

"But they know you were kidnapped by him, right?" Rosie asked.

"They know Bradley and Sean found me at his office," she said. "They know that I'd been fighting with him and that I showed trace elements of drugs in my system when they tested my blood."

"Well that should be enough," Stanley said. "That should get him locked up nice and tight for a while."

"I certainly hope so," Bradley said. "But whatever happens, I know that Mary will do her best on the stand."

Mary felt her stomach tighten. She just prayed her best would be good enough.

The oven timer went off. Rosie picked up some oven mitts, walked across the kitchen and pulled a steaming casserole dish of lasagna out of the oven. She placed it on a waiting trivet, slipped the mitts off and looked up at the group of adults staring ravenously at the dish. Laughing, she picked up the salad bowl and brought it to the table. "We have to let it sit for at least ten minutes," she said. "Or when it's cut it will be runny."

"I don't mind runny," Ian said, following her to the table, but looking longingly over his shoulder. "Runny is fine."

Stanley adjusted the waistband on his pants and nodded. "Can't say I argue with Ian," he said. "Ten minutes seems like an awful long time to wait."

Shaking her finger at them, she walked back and entered ten minutes into the oven timer. "You will both wait for ten minutes," she said. "And no one will starve in the meantime because we can eat the salad and garlic bread."

Bradley reached over and picked up the bowl of bread. "Where would you like me to put this, Rosie?" he asked.

Smiling at him, she nodded happily. "See, that's how it should be," she said. "Over there, next to the salad, Bradley."

He put the bowl down and sat in a chair next to Ian.

"Kiss up," Ian whispered.

Bradley grinned at him. "Just wait and see who gets the first serving of lasagna," he whispered back.

Chapter Twenty-five

A few hours later, Bradley and Mary stood on her back porch looking up at the hundreds of stars in the night sky. With his arm around her shoulders, he pulled her closer and gently kissed the top of her head. "You were amazing today in court," he said. "I meant to mention that to you earlier, but with the testimony and everything, it slipped my mind."

She looked up at him, confused. "I was great?" she asked. "But I didn't do anything."

"You stood up to your fears, you faced down Gary Copper and you let him know he couldn't intimidate you anymore," he replied, kissing her forehead. "You were amazing."

She smiled and shrugged. "Well, with all the support I had from you, Sean and Ian," she said, "I realized Gary really couldn't do anything to hurt me and we were finally going to have our day in court and take him down."

The smile on Bradley's face dropped. "If we can take him down," he finally said.

"You don't think there's enough evidence to lock him away?" she asked. "Even if the prosecution can't use the frozen bodies, she can certainly use the fact that he lied about Jeannine and buried her under his wife's name. And he falsely signed a death certificate. There has to be something there."

He nodded. "You're right," he said. "But I'd like to be able to put him away for more than forgery."

"I agree," she said. "I'd like to see him locked up in a dark place for a long, long time."

He slipped his hand to her shoulder and turned her to face him. "Here I am, standing with the most beautiful woman in the world in a dark private place with stars glistening overhead and I'm not kissing her senseless," he said, his voice low and his eyes searching her face. "What would Stanley say?"

Giggling, she reached down and pretended to adjust the waistband of her slacks. "Well, I ain't saying I know what he'd say, and I ain't saying I don't know what he'd say," she said, trying to mimic Stanley's voice. "But I can tell you fer sure…"

She paused and the grin left her face as she met his eyes. "I can tell you," she repeated in her own voice. "That being kissed senseless is something that she would enjoy very much."

He pulled her to him and lowered his head slowly. "Did I mention how much I love you?" he asked, his voice husky.

She wrapped her arms around his neck. "Show me."

He crushed his lips against her and tightened his embrace, molding her body against his. He wanted to show her, needed to show her, how much he loved her and how essential she was to his life.

She sighed with pleasure as he deepened their kiss and buried her hands in his hair, to pull him even closer. This was where she belonged, in his arms, in his embrace and she never wanted to leave.

He slid one hand up her shoulder, along her neck and finally cradled her face in his palm. Barely lifting his head from her lips, he looked down on the face he'd come to love more than life itself. Her eyes shining with her love for him. Her lips swollen from their kisses. And her smile, tender, sexy and uniquely Mary. "How did I ever get so lucky?" he asked softly.

Her smile widened. "Obviously you've led an exceptional life," she purred, and then pulled his head down to indulge in another heart-pounding series of kisses.

A few minutes later, Mary laid her head on his chest, her breath coming out in puffs of steam in the below freezing temperatures. "Wow," she whispered. "Just wow."

He laid his cheek on her head and just held her in his arms. "You pack quite a punch, Mary O'Reilly," he murmured.

She nuzzled closer. "I do?" she asked, pleased with herself.

She could feel him nod. "Oh, yes, you certainly do," he replied. "Are you sure we have to wait until June?"

She laughed softly and punched him gently in his side. "Yes, and stop tempting me," she said, leaning back to meet his eyes. "Besides, I want Clarissa as my flower girl."

He inhaled sharply, nodded and waited a moment before he answered. "That would be…" he began, his voice thick with emotion. "That would be perfect."

"But Stanley, I was sure you said it was Ian who was snoring," Rosie was saying as Mary and Bradley came back inside the house.

"Well, I didn't say he did and I didn't say he didn't," they both heard Stanley respond.

Mary turned and muffled her laughter against Bradley's chest. He wrapped his arms around her and looked down at her, smiling at the same joke. "If nothing else, he's consistent," Bradley whispered.

Mary nodded. "Yes, he is."

Mary stepped back and took Bradley's hand. "Well, let's get back into the real world."

They entered the front room, their hands clasped together. "What's this I hear about snoring?" Bradley asked.

Stanley growled. "Ain't nothing," he grumbled. "A man can't make a little noise while he sleeps without the whole world making a federal case about it."

"Oh, it was a federal case," Ian teased. "Didn't we tell you Homeland Security stopped by this morning because they thought we were using explosive devices in the house?"

Stanley glared at Ian. "Aye, and once we invited them in and they witnessed your amazing ability, they said they were going to Congress and see if they can get permission to use you as a national weapon," he continued.

"You ain't funny," Stanley said, folding his arms over his chest. "You ain't funny t'all."

Ian chuckled. "Rosie, you wouldn't mind honeymooning in Washington, D.C., would you?"

Rosie laughed. "Well, I'd be married to a national hero," she said. "That would be exciting."

Mary and Bradley sat down on the couch. "More than a national hero," Mary added. "A superhero with amazing powers."

"Ah, you have it right there, Mary," Ian said, a mischievous twinkle in his eyes. "During the day he's mild-mannered Stanley Wagner, salesman of pens and paperclips. But once darkness falls and the people of Freeport take to their beds, he turns into Snoreman."

Stanley bit back a smile. "T'ain't funny, at all."

"Does he have a costume?" Bradley asked.

Ian nodded. "Aye, a nightshirt and cap," he said. "Like Wee Willy Winkie."

"Who?" Mary asked.

Turning to her, shock evident on his face, he shook his head. "No, you can't be telling me you've never heard of Wee Willy Winkie?" he asked. "And what did your mother read to you at bedtime?"

She shrugged. "*One Fish, Two Fish, Red Fish, Blue Fish?*"

"Ah, you've missed a bit of great literature," he said. "Now, let me see if I can remember it. 'Wee

163

Willie Winkie rins through the toon, Upstairs an' doon stairs in his night-gown, Tirlin' at the window, crying at the lock, Are the weans in their bed, for it's now ten o'clock?'"

"Why don't you repeat it so we can understand it?" Stanley grumbled. "You're in America now, we speak American."

"Stanley, we don't speak American," Rosie corrected him gently. "We speak English."

"Whatever," Stanley grumbled. "It ain't what he just said."

Bradley chuckled. "Well, it just so happens that I have an extra guest room at my house," he said. "And I'd be happy to have Stanley stay with me tonight. If that's alright with all of you."

"Aye, it's fine with me," Ian said. "And, if you don't mind, I'll come along and take your couch. I'd like to do a quick visit to Stanley's house tonight and see if we can't meet his charming first wife."

He turned to Mary. "You don't mind if all of the menfolk desert you, do you?"

"No, I think Rosie and I would like some girl time anyway," she said. "We'll see you in the morning."

In a few minutes, they had all said their goodbyes and the men were pulling their cars away from the curb.

"Mary," Rosie said tentatively. "I was wondering if we could take a little drive tonight too?"

Mary nodded. "Rosie, I was hoping you'd say that."

164

Chapter Twenty-six

Stanley unlocked his front door and the three men entered together. Stanley walked in first, followed by Ian and finally Bradley.

"So, where did you see her?" Ian asked, his voice low.

Stanley motioned with his head. "Over here," he said and they followed him through the living room and into the kitchen. "I was heating up some milk to have with some of Rosie's strawberry rhubarb pie…"

"Strawberry rhubarb pie," Ian interrupted, turning toward the refrigerator. "Do you have any left?"

"I don't know," Stanley grumbled. "Can you just concentrate on what we're trying to do here?"

Nodding, Ian turned back toward Stanley. "Sorry, you were saying…"

"So, I cut myself a piece of pie and out of the corner of my eye I see something," he said. "Something glowing, walking from my office to my bedroom."

Bradley walked to the hall and peered down it both ways. "Well, there isn't a window nearby that would be able to cast a reflection from a passing car. So, that can be ruled out."

"Yeah, I was looking for that on the second night," he said, "looking for a reasonable explanation. But when I saw her again, I knew there tweren't no explanation, there was just a ghost."

Walking into his office, they could see the oversized black trash bag in the middle of the room. "Rosie's making me clean it out," he explained. "I have to throw most of my stuff away."

"Now, that's scary," Ian said. "Why is she making you do it?"

Leaning against the doorjamb, Stanley sighed. "After tossing my stuff out of my bedroom drawer, Verna turned to me and said, 'Don't forget.' Rosie figures she was looking for something I couldn't remember and Verna couldn't find because of the mess. She figured if I cleaned things up, it would help me remember."

Bradley stepped inside the room and looked at all of the piles. He picked up a newspaper dated November 1999 and nodded. "When did Verna die?" he asked.

"About fifteen years ago," Stanley replied.

He picked up the next paper in the pile, dated December 1999. "And when was the last time you cleaned this room out?" he continued.

Stanley grumbled and grabbed both papers from him. "About fifteen years ago," he admitted. "But there's some important stuff in here. I might need the stuff in here. There's articles from magazines I need to clip out and file."

Ian walked over to the file cabinet and pulled open the top drawer. There were a number of hanging files with one or two thin manila files in each. "Stanley, when was the last time you actually opened this file cabinet?" he asked.

Stanley sighed deeply. "About fifteen years ago," he admitted. "But I meant…"

Ian walked over and put his arm around Stanley's shoulders. "Yeah, I know," he said. "But I think Rosie's right, you're going to find the clue to what's bothering Verna here in this room. And you want to set things right with your first wife, before you go ahead and take on a second."

"I suppose…" Stanley stopped mid-sentence as a glow from the hallway caught their eye.

They hurried out of the room in time to see Verna float down the hall and into Stanley's room.

"Bradley, can you see her too?" Ian asked.

Bradley nodded. "Yeah, I see her," he replied as they all walked slowly down the hall to Stanley's bedroom.

They found her at his dresser pulling things out of his drawers again.

"Ask her what she's looking for," Ian whispered. "Ask her what you weren't supposed to forget."

Stanley took a tentative step forward. "Um, Verna, honey," he began.

The ghost paused and turned her head to look at him.

"I know you want me to remember something or find something, and I'm cleaning my office, hoping it will help," he explained. "But I'm sorry, sweetheart; I can't remember what you want me to remember."

One small tear slid down from Verna's eye and left a trail down her cheek. "Stanley," she said slowly. "Don't forget."

And then she disappeared.

\# \# \# \#

Mary pulled the Roadster into Rosie's driveway and shifted into park. She turned to Rosie sitting next to her. "Are you sure you want to go in there?" she asked. "We could wait until Ian and Bradley are available."

Shaking her head, Rosie looked at the house and clasped her hands together tightly. "I have a feeling it won't appear if there are men in the house," she said quietly. "I think we would just be wasting our time with Ian or Bradley or even Stanley here. I think we need to face it."

She turned to Mary. "You don't mind do you?" she asked. "I mean, it was quite terrifying, but I thought with you here, it wouldn't be so bad."

Mary placed her hand over Rosie's hands. "I don't mind at all," she said. "And I've faced terrifying ghosts before. Let's go in and see if he's man enough to stand up to two strong women."

The night was still and the street was dark. All of Rosie's neighbors seemed to have already turned in for the night. They crept forward to the front door, the key clutched in Rosie's hand. She inserted it into the lock, and turned slowly. Her hand grasping the doorknob, she pushed it open carefully, gazing around the room before going inside.

Even shadowed in darkness, the house seemed peaceful. Cheerful and bright afghans were tossed over her couch and upholstered chairs, inviting someone to curl up and get comfortable. The scent of cinnamon and cloves wafted in the air. Porcelain figures of angels were perched throughout the house, inviting all visitors to relax under their watchful eye.

Rosie entered the house and Mary followed close behind. "Should I turn on the light?" Rosie asked Mary.

"Have you ever seen or heard anything in this room?" Mary responded.

"No. Only in the bedroom," she replied.

"Then I think it's safe for us to turn on the light in here," Mary said. "But a dimmer light would probably be better."

Rosie turned on a small lamp that rested next to her couch. The soft light made the home seem even more warm and welcoming.

"Well, it doesn't feel like a scary place," Mary said, shrugging off her coat. "I've always loved your home."

A smile spread over Rosie's face and she sighed contentedly as she looked around her room. "I needed to make it a warm and comforting place," she explained. "I needed to make it a place where I felt safe and secure."

She shook her head. "And it always has," her voice cracked, "until now."

Mary took a deep breath. "Well, let's go and change that, okay?"

Rosie nodded and together they walked through the house to the bedroom. Rosie put her hand on the doorknob. "Do you think he just went away because I left last night?" she asked hopefully.

"No, I don't think it's going to be that easy," Mary replied. "Besides, you wouldn't have resolution and you would always wonder if he was going to come back. You need to face him and find out who he is and why he's haunting you."

She took a deep breath and nodded, then she pushed the door open. The room was still, with the bed unmade, the chaise lounge pushed up against the closet door and the television still running. Rosie turned apologetically to Mary. "I haven't been back since I ran out last night," she said. "I still had some things at your place."

Mary put her arm on the older woman's shoulder. "That's okay," she said. "I wouldn't have come back here alone either. I know you have the courage to face whatever this is, but you needed time to develop a plan."

Rosie nodded. "So, what's our plan?" she asked.

Mary smiled. "Well, I suppose we need to find out who your visitor is before we can decide what you need to say to him," she suggested. "So, why don't you get ready for bed, just like you did both of those other times? And I'll sit quietly in the corner over there."

Mary pointed to the far corner of the room, away from the bed and the closet, a place where she could watch the whole room from a clear vantage point.

Rosie nodded. "That sounds like a good plan," she agreed.

Mary pulled a chair to the corner of the room and sat back while Rosie performed her nightly rituals. "Can I talk to you?" she called from the bathroom.

"I think you might want to act as if you're alone," Mary responded. "Especially as it gets closer to the time your visitor normally arrives."

Rosie looked at the little clock on the bathroom counter. "Okay, we have about fifteen minutes," she said. "I'll get into bed now."

Rosie walked across the room, dressed in a nightgown over her clothes. She looked over at Mary with a sheepish smile. "Just in case we have to leave in a hurry," she whispered.

Climbing into bed, she allowed the television to stay on and illuminate the room, but turned off the rest of the lights. She pounded her pillow a couple of times and then laid her head down and feigned sleep.

Chapter Twenty-seven

Mary settled back in the chair and waited. The sound of the news reporter on the television was just loud enough for Mary to hear the report on today's trial. Reporting on Bradley's comment about two bodies found in the freezer and the judge disallowing the information to be shared with the jury, the reporter went on to speak about Bradley.

"We asked a number of Sycamore residents if they remembered Officer Alden when he served their community on the police force. Most who remembered him, described a hard-working, civic-minded individual who took protecting the citizens of the community seriously. There was one comment by a young man who Alden had arrested when he was teenager who considered Alden a troublemaker and a busybody. Overall, the people here are sympathetic to the young police officer and his quest to obtain justice in the death of his wife."

Mary smiled and nodded. *Good! Even though public support won't win the trial, it will be nice for Bradley to know he's got backing.*

The lighting in the room changed as the news program went to commercial. Suddenly the room was darker and the sound of the television muted. Mary quickly looked over to the closet door and her heart raced as she watched it slowly open.

Game time!

As the closet opening increased, the atmosphere in the room changed. Shadows grew and the room was encased in a fog-like gloom. The air seemed heavy and oppressive. The noise from the television and the street outside was muted. Mary was on high alert, waiting and watching to see what came out of the closet.

Like watching a shadow figure on a wall, at first she only saw a hand, gnarled and elongated, with fingernails that seemed more claw-like than human. The arm that followed was also long and narrow, encased in a black sleeve that hung loosely from the shoulder, as if the clothing was too large for the frame. Then the body floated out of its hiding place. Bent at the shoulders and waist, the figure could have been tall if it had been straight. Its head moved furtively, searching portions of the room, but it didn't turn toward Mary. Instead it glided toward Rosie's bed, silently and stealthily.

Mary stood, making no noise as she straightened from her chair. She moved quickly, wanting to protect Rosie before the specter frightened her again, yet waiting for the best moment to confront it.

The ghost, more shadow than substance, seemed to grow taller as it loomed over Rosie. Mary thought she could hear a slow, rhythmic breath being expelled from its mouth as it stood next to the bed and watched over the woman. Then it started to levitate and move toward the bed.

"Rosie," Mary shouted.

Rosie slipped from the bed and faced the ghost.

Mary ran forward and shut the closet door, then rushed to Rosie's side.

The shadow raced around the room, knocking pictures from the wall and knickknacks from shelves. Then it stopped in a shadow in the far corner of the room, facing them.

"Who are you?" Mary called, her arm protectively around Rosie. "What do you want?"

Lifting its arm, it pointed a narrow finger at Rosie.

"Sorry, you can't have her," Mary said. "She belongs to this world and you belong to the next. You have no power over her. Now, go away."

Mary's words seemed to enrage the ghost, whose shadow was growing larger and stretching up from the wall onto the ceiling.

Rosie gasped softly and hid her face in Mary's shoulder until she heard the crackle of laughter coming from the ghost. She understood the laughter was directed at her. He thought he was winning. He thought she was weak. He liked to see her weak and cowering.

She took a deep breath and stepped away from Mary's protective shelter. She moved forward into the room, toward the ghost. "You don't belong here," she said, her voice quavering at first, but becoming stronger. "This is my room, mine. I created it. It reflects me and no scary, mean and ugly thing belongs here."

The shadow seemed to shrink slightly.

"You have no control over me," she continued. "You are nothing, only a shadow."

She continued to move forward. "I won't let you scare me any longer," she said.

She stepped over to the light switch next to the bedroom door, but before she could turn it on, the closet door flew open with a bang and the ghost flew inside, slamming it shut behind itself.

Rosie switched on the light, turned to Mary and exhaled deeply. "Well, if that wasn't one of the scariest moments of my life, I don't know what else is," she said.

Mary moved forward quickly and embraced Rosie. "You were so brave," she said. "I was so proud of you."

Rosie beamed. "Really? You were proud of me?"

Nodding, Mary hugged her again. "It took a lot of courage to confront that thing," she said. "To stand up for yourself. You were amazing."

"So, do you think it's gone?" Rosie asked.

Shaking her head, Mary met her friend's eyes. "No, not yet," she said. "But we've got him on the run. I don't think he's quite as sure about you as he was when he first came out of the closet. But I think it's going to take a couple more conversations with him."

"Why is he doing this?" Rosie asked. "Who is he?"

"Those are the very things we need to find out in order to make him leave you alone," she said. "But that can wait until tomorrow night. Let's pack some things up for you and go back to my place for a good night's sleep."

Chapter Twenty-eight

"The court calls Mary O'Reilly to the witness stand," the court clerk announced the next morning.

Mary stood and walked forward to the witness stand. She placed her hand on the Bible.

"Do you swear to tell the truth, the whole truth and nothing but the truth, so help you God?" the clerk asked.

Mary nodded her head. "Yes, I do," she agreed.

"You may be seated," the clerk said.

Mary sat and watched Lydia walk forward. "Ms. O'Reilly, can you tell the jury what you do for a living?" she asked.

"I'm a private investigator," she replied.

"And what makes you qualified to be a private investigator?" she asked.

"I'm a former Chicago police officer, a former member of the vice squad and I was up for promotion to detective status," she replied. "I also graduated with honors in Criminal Justice from the University of Illinois."

"Can you tell us why you were not promoted to detective status?" she asked.

Nodding, Mary sat a little taller in her chair. "I was shot in the line of duty," she explained. "And I was given permanent disability status."

"Ms. O'Reilly, isn't it true that the reason you were shot was because you threw yourself in front of a drug dealer who was going to shoot another officer?" Lydia asked.

"I was only doing my job," Mary replied, uncomfortable with the question.

"You received an accommodation for service above and beyond the call of duty," Lydia said. "Didn't you?"

Mary nodded. "Yes, I did," she said.

"And isn't it true that you died on the operating table because your injury was so severe?"

Mary glanced over to Sean and saw regret pass across his face. She took a deep breath and faced Lydia. "Yes, I flat-lined on the table and technically I died. But as you can see," she smiled at the jury. "I got better."

"I know you are uncomfortable with this line of questioning, Ms. O'Reilly," Lydia said. "But I want the jury to understand not only what kind of officer you were, but what kind of person you are."

Mary nodded.

"Why did you decide to investigate Jeannine Alden's murder?" she asked.

"Back in December, Chief Alden and I were working on an infant snatching case that led us to Chicago," Mary explained. "During that investigation, Chief Alden was shot and ended up in Cook County Hospital. While we were there, I received information from a source who wishes to remain anonymous that his wife had died at the hospital. Chief Alden had explained his search for his wife and his daughter to me, and I knew he still hoped to find them alive. But, as a police investigator, you understand that you should follow up on any lead. I decided to follow up."

"Did you tell Chief Alden?"

Mary shook her head. "No, because the source asked me not to divulge their identity and because if it was a false lead, I didn't want to cause Chief Alden any extra concern while he was recuperating from his injury."

"What did you discover?" she asked.

"We discovered that Jeannine had been forcibly taken from her home," she said, "but we still didn't know the identity of the perpetrator. At that point, I decided to work with Chief Alden and see if we could set up a similar scenario, using his home as a base and see if we couldn't encourage the criminal to repeat his crime."

"Did you follow police procedure in doing the investigation?" she asked.

Mary nodded. "We had the Freeport Police Department and the Chicago Police Department monitoring the status of the investigation at all times," she said. "Because we didn't want word of the investigation to leak, we decided not to alert the local authorities until it was time to bring them in for the arrest."

"Who worked with you on the case?"

"Professor Ian MacDougal from the University of Edinburgh," Mary replied. "He has a fellowship through the University of Chicago to study various kinds of police procedures."

"What did you and Professor MacDougal do?" Lydia asked.

"We posed as a newlywed couple who was moving into the area," she explained. "We wanted to represent some of the same traits as Chief Alden and Jeannine, so we spread the word that I was expecting our first child."

"What was the conclusion of your investigation?"

"We had several suspects and we had a theory that Jeannine had been drugged by using food," she said. "So we brought all of the neighbors together for a brunch. During the brunch, only one guest had access to the food and that was Gary Copper. We started the meal and within a half hour, all of the guests were unconscious and I had been taken from the home and brought to Gary's office. He had a subterranean room with a stainless steel door that was locked from the outside. When I awoke, Gary told me that he was going to keep me there and that he was going to rape me."

"What did you do?" Lydia asked.

"I was still under the influence of the drug," Mary said. "I begged him to let me go and I said that I would fight him. He calmly stated that he had a twilight drug he was going to use on me, so I would be awake, but unable to fight him. He injected me with the drug…"

She paused, her voice shaking and took a deep breath. "He started to touch me and he kept telling me that I was going to like it," she said, shuddering. "He was repulsive."

"What happened next?"

"I fought him," Mary said. "Somehow I was able to push him off of me and keep him from raping me. He had me cornered when Chief Alden broke in and rescued me."

"Did Dr. Copper tell you why he wanted to kidnap you?" she asked.

"He wanted a willing wife and a child," she said. "He told me that his wife was going to leave him when she found out that he had been videotaping his female patients when they were under the influence of anesthesia. He told me that he didn't let her leave him. That she was still waiting for him at home."

"Did you believe that your life was threatened and he would have raped you if Chief Alden had not arrived when he had?" Lydia asked.

Mary nodded her head. "Yes, I believe that he intended to hold me as a prisoner for as long as he was able," she said. "When he held me captive, he confessed he had held Jeannine as a prisoner too."

"Do you believe that Gary Copper is the reason Jeannine Alden is dead?"

There was no hesitation in Mary's response. "Yes, if he had not kidnapped her, held her as a prisoner and drugged her, she would be alive today," Mary said. "He might not have injected her with the medication that ultimately caused her heart attack, but she would not have been in that circumstance, without her medical records, if he had not decided to pursue his depraved scheme."

Lydia nodded and smiled at Mary. "Thank you, Ms. O'Reilly, she said. "No further questions."

"Mr. Thanner, do you want to cross-examine the witness?" the judge asked.

Greg nodded. "Yes, I most certainly do," he said.

He pushed his arms against the table to stand and reached forward for another folder. He flipped it open and scanned a document. Then he moved forward to stand in front of the witness stand. "Ms. O'Reilly," he said. "You were given permanent disability from the Chicago Police Department, is that correct?"

She nodded. "Yes, it is."

"And was this because of a physical injury that would prohibit you from continuing your career?" he asked.

"No, it wasn't," she replied.

"Indeed it wasn't," he concurred with a mocking smile. "You were offered disability because of some psychological issues you had after the shooting. Weren't you?"

Mary nodded. "Yes, but that's not unusual. Being shot is very traumatic and, in my case, the force honorably offered me disability pension."

"Was that because of your outstanding record, or because you claimed to your psychologist that you could see and talk to ghosts?" he asked.

Well, crap. Mary thought.

"Objection," Lydia called. "Ms. O'Reilly's personal medical records have no bearing on this case."

"Your honor, it's basically Ms. O'Reilly's word against my client's word," he said. "I think her state of mind has every bearing on the case."

Nodding, the judge rapped her gavel. "I'll allow it," she said. "Continue."

Thanner turned back to Mary. "Now, Ms. O'Reilly, please answer my question. Were you given a permanent disability status because of your ability to see and speak with ghosts?"

Taking a deep breath, Mary met Thanner's eyes. "Yes," she said. "Although I passed all other portions of both my medical and psych evaluation, the Chicago Police Department did not know how to evaluate someone with my new abilities."

"So, you don't deny you talk to ghosts?" he asked, a smirk appearing on his face.

Mary was quiet for a moment as she gathered her thoughts. She had watched the little boy follow Thanner for several days of the trial. Every time Thanner stood, the little ghost followed him. Always standing next to him. "Who are you?" Mary finally asked.

"I'm Garth, Greg's twin brother," the boy responded with a bright smile. "You can see me?"

Mary nodded.

"I'm sorry, Ms. O'Reilly," Thanner said. "Are you having a psychological episode right now? I am Greg Thanner."

Mary shook her head and smiled at him. "I'm sorry, I wasn't addressing you, Mr. Thanner," she said. "I was asking your twin brother, Garth, his name."

Thanner turned white and stumbled back several steps. "What the hell kind of game are you playing, O'Reilly?" he yelled.

Mary shook her head. "No game, Mr. Thanner, I'm under oath and I am answering your questions."

"How did you know my brother died?"

Mary leaned forward in her seat. "He just told me," she replied. "And if you read the report more thoroughly, you'll find the psychologist did not find me abnormal or crazy. She actually found me quite healthy considering what I'd been through. They just didn't know how to categorize this ability. My psychologist actually believed I could see and speak with ghosts."

"Do you expect the jury to believe you?"

Mary nodded. "I really hope they do," she said. "Do you believe me?"

"Anyone could have researched me and found out my brother died," he said. "Does emotional manipulation also fall under your talents?"

"Objection," Lydia called. "Badgering the witness."

"Sustained," the judged agreed. "Mr. Thanner, you called in question the witness' ability to see ghosts. She countered by mentioning a ghost that is evidently in this courtroom. Do you have a follow up?"

He glared at Mary. "I'm not going to ask you how my brother died, because you would have learned that when you did your research," he said.

"I'm not trying to play any games with you, Mr. Thanner," Mary said. "But, as you said, this whole case lies in the jury believing me or not. You have just set me up to appear as a nutcase so you can win this trial. I'm under oath and I was a sworn law enforcement officer. Even though it is very uncomfortable for me to admit what I can do in a public venue and, of course, encounter the ridicule that will go with it, I will do it in order to ensure that Gary Copper ends up behind bars."

"What would you have me do, Ms. O'Reilly?" he asked.

"Your job," she said simply. "Ask me a question."

"What did my brother and I call each other as nicknames when we were growing up?" he asked.

Mary paused for a moment and then smiled at Thanner. "Well, you called each other G-men because both of your names, obviously, began with G and you liked the FBI," she said, and her smile split into a wide grin. "But Garth said he also called you 'Tubbers,' a name you weren't as fond of."

His jaw dropped and he stared at her. "How…?" he began, his face turned toward the witness stand, then he caught himself, took a deep breath and moved toward the jury box. "Wrong, Ms. O'Reilly. I guess your parlor tricks don't work well in court. So much for your demonstration."

"But…but that's what Garth told me. That's the truth," she replied.

He shrugged. "Good try, Ms. O'Reilly," he said. "Now let's get back to the trial."

She turned to the judge. "He's lying," she insisted.

"I'm sorry, Ms. O'Reilly, you need to answer the questions," the judge replied.

Thanner approached her again. "And now, Ms. O'Reilly," he asked, "what is your current relationship with Chief Alden?"

"We are engaged to be married," she said, still shaken from Thanner's lie.

He nodded. "And the bullet you took in the line of duty," he said. "I understand that bullet was aimed at your brother, Sean. Is that correct?"

Mary nodded. "Yes, Sean didn't see the drug dealer with the gun. He wouldn't have had a chance to defend himself, so I blocked the shot."

"It seems to me, Ms. O'Reilly, that you will go to any lengths for the people you love," he said. "No further questions, your honor."

Chapter Twenty-nine

Clarissa sat in class and, as it got closer to the end of the day, the knots in her stomach got tighter and tighter. She had never walked home alone, actually never walked home at all. They lived at the very edge of the school boundaries, so she always had a ride or took the bus with her mother, rather than walk the two miles.

The good news was that her mother had to work late, so Clarissa had plenty of time to get home. She looked out the classroom window, and it wasn't raining or snowing, so she wouldn't get too cold. This might not be such a bad thing after all. She would just think about it as an adventure.

The bell rang and Clarissa grabbed her coat from the back of her chair and quickly shoved her personal belongings into her backpack. She looked around, panicked; wanting to be sure she left the school with a large group of students. She hadn't made any friends, but she'd learned quickly enough that if you were walking alone, you were a target.

She walked alongside a group of girls from her class, acting as though she were part of their close-knit group. They didn't go out the front door of the school; the door she was used to exiting in order to meet Mrs. Gunderson. Instead, they walked out a side door and cut across the frozen playground outside the school. They stopped for a moment by the playground equipment and Clarissa leaned against the cold metal pole of the swing set and waited for them.

"You need something?" one of the girls asked her.

Clarissa shook her head, trying to come up with a viable excuse to stay with them. "No, I'm just trying to stay away from Tony," she lied, naming one of the unpopular boys in their class. "He sent me a note today and said he likes me."

"Oh, girl, that's gross," another girl said. "That boy is nasty. You don't want to go near him."

Clarissa nodded. "Yeah, so I thought I'd walk home another way, so he can't find me."

The first girl nodded. "Sure, you can hang with us," she said. "We always walk home together. Come on; let's get out of here before he sees you."

They hurried out of the school yard and crossed the street, taking several residential streets and then cutting through a gangway of a large apartment complex to end up on a busy street that didn't look familiar.

"Where are we?" Clarissa asked.

"On Broadway," the second girl responded.

"Broadway?" Clarissa asked. "I don't remember that street."

"Maybe if you keep walking for a little while you'll see something you remember," the girl suggested.

Clarissa nodded and continued to walk with them.

They walked a few more blocks and the girls stopped at a major intersection to separate and go their own ways. Clarissa looked around at the busy streets, the traffic lights and the small stores surrounding her. Nothing looked familiar. Nothing looked like the way to her apartment.

One of the girls turned to her. "You going home or you staying here?" she asked.

"I…I don't know where I am," she confessed.

"What's your address?"

Clarissa repeated her address and the girl shook her head. "That ain't nowhere around here," she said. "You went the wrong way when you came out of the school."

"What should I do?" Clarissa asked.

"You gotta walk back to the school and go the other way."

Clarissa took a deep shaky breath. *All the way back to the school? I don't even know if I can find it.*

"And don't let no cops find you wandering around," the girl added. "If they find out you're lost, they gonna lock your momma up in jail for not taking care of you."

"Really?" Clarissa asked.

"Uh huh," the girl replied. "And they'll put you in some home for children. It happened to my cousin."

Clarissa nodded silently. There was no way she was going to get caught by the police and make her mother go to jail.

"Which way back to the school?" she asked.

The girl shook her head. "You is in trouble if you don't even know that," she said, but she pointed back down the street and gave her directions. "You go back to that corner there, see, and then you turn left. Then you walk three more blocks, turn right and cross the street and then go down that street two more blocks. You should see the playground. But don't go back by the school. Those gangs hang out there after school and if they catch you, they gonna hurt you. So, you stay across the street from the school. And don't go into no alleys because they is bad men in those alleys and they gonna hurt you too. Understand?"

Her heart thudding in her chest, Clarissa nodded. "Thank you," she whispered, her mouth suddenly dry.

"I sure hope I see you in school tomorrow," the girl said. "I sure hope you make it home."

"Thank you," Clarissa repeated. "Me too."

By the time Clarissa had made it to the second turn, it was beginning to get a little dark. She pulled her mittens out of her pockets and pulled them over her hands, as the wind picked up and the night air was colder.

"If I can make it back to the school, I'll be fine," she whispered to herself.

Following the girl's directions, she felt her heart lift when she actually saw the playground about a block in the distance. She made it! She began to cross the street to head to the playground, when she saw the squad car turn the corner. Her heart dropped. She couldn't let them find her; she didn't want her mother to go to jail.

She looked around quickly, trying to decide where to hide and saw a narrow gangway between two tall apartment buildings. She rushed past a row of scraggy hedges, down a broken sidewalk and into the narrow passage.

A sour smell assailed her nose as soon as she got close to the area. It smelled like the alleyway behind their apartment, next to the bar. The ground beneath her shoes was sticky and wet, she felt her stomach turn. This place was gross.

She entered the tall and narrow gangway. It was like entering a dark cave. There were no lights, only a series of steps that led up to the back porches of the apartments. Large garbage cans sat next to the steps, trash scattered all around them. As she moved forward, a large piece of newspaper skittered across the ground. She stopped and stared; something big and brown slipped from underneath the paper into the shadows underneath the steps. She froze. There were rats in this place.

She stepped back and heard a rustling sound in the garbage can behind her. Jumping forward, she ran to the edge of the gangway and looked around. She couldn't go into the gangway, there were too many rats. She peeked past the brick building and saw the police car slow down in front of the building.

She ducked down, hidden by the scraggly bushes and the shadows of the building.

Waiting, her heart pounding, her breath coming out in tiny gasps that puffed out as white smoke in the cold air, she could hear the sound of rustling move even closer. She'd seen rat bites on some of the kids at school. Some of them even had to go to the hospital and get shots. She knew her mother couldn't take her to a hospital. Could someone die of a rat bite?

Hearing the sound of a car moving up the street, she knew the police car had moved on. She started to stand up when she felt the thump of something hitting her backpack. She jumped forward, turning quickly, as a large rat fell to the ground at her feet. She gasped and clamped her hand over her mouth to stop herself from screaming out loud. Eyes wide in terror, she darted out from the gangway and ran up the street, away from the police car and away from the rats.

Finally, minutes later, she was out of breath and her lungs were aching from the exertion. She knew she was lost. Knew she had run away from the playground and away from the police. She looked around and found herself in front of a huge building that looked like a castle. Tall towers of stone with colored glass windows stood on either side of the large wooden doors. The steps up to the doors were white and bigger than any steps she had ever seen.

She looked up and down the street, what could she do now? She started to sit on the large steps, when the sound of an approaching car startled her. *The police!* she thought. Making her mind up quickly, she ran up the stairs to the heavy wooden door and, using all her weight, pushed it open.

The inside of the building was dimly lit, with only the soft light of candles and dimmed recessed lighting illuminating the large room before her. She walked forward, her shoes clicking against the polished wood floor. The air smelled a little funny, like wax and...something spicy. Row after row of long pews filled the room and at the very front was a white marble altar with a large crucifix hanging high on the wall behind it.

Not a castle, a church, she thought, although she couldn't remember any of the churches in Freeport being this big or fancy.

She stopped about halfway to the altar, slipped into a pew and sat on the padded upholstery. She looked up at the face on the crucifix and then around at all of the statues and paintings of the saints. They all seemed to be staring at her, waiting for something.

"I'm lost," she whispered. "God, will you please help me?"

A door at the back of the altar opened and a dark-robed priest entered the chapel.

Will he help me? Clarissa wondered. *Or will he call the police?*

He moved across the altar silently, meaningfully, to the pulpit. Once there he searched it and pulled out a manila folder. He didn't seem to notice her, so she sat silently and just watched him. She felt safe in the church, safe and warm. Her feet were tingling because they weren't cold anymore. She looked at the padded bench. If she could just lie down for a minute and rest, then she was sure she'd feel better.

Slipping her backpack off, she placed it next to her on the pew and lay down, using her backpack as a pillow. She yawned deeply as the warmth from the room seeped into her tired and cold body. Just a few minutes, she thought sleepily, and then she would walk the rest of the way home.

Chapter Thirty

Clarissa felt someone shaking her shoulder, trying to wake her up. "Is it morning already?" she muttered.

"Ah, no, tikna, it is just evening," a man's accented voice replied.

Immediately waking, Clarissa gasped in surprise and tried to dart away. The man had dark hair, an olive complexion and thick stubble on his cheeks and chin. He was wearing a brightly colored button-down shirt under a canvas jacket and a kerchief tied around his neck. When he smiled two gold teeth glistened in the candlelight of the church.

She tried to move back, but the man held on to her shoulder. "There is no need to be afraid, chavvi," he said. "Mami Nadja, you know her, yes?"

Clarissa nodded mutely.

He nodded and smiled. "She send me," he said, nodding his head as he explained. "She say 'Meri, you go find Clarissa and help her go home', so I come to kahngeri, church, and I find you sleeping."

"How did Mami know I was here?" she asked, her eyes wide in wonder.

"Ah, she is…Drabarni… She speaks with angels," he said. "They tell her you need help to go home. No? Is that right?"

"Yes, I was praying for angels to help me," she admitted. "My daddy used to say that angels were always watching out for us."

"Your daddy, he is a smart man," Meri said.

Sighing, Clarissa looked down at the pew. "My daddy's dead," she said.

"Ah, tikna, I am sorry," he said. "I too lost my father when I was little. It is hard for a child to grow up without a father."

A tear escaped Clarissa's eye, but she quickly wiped it away. "It's hard for my mommy," she said, taking a deep breath. "Daddy used to take care of lots of things for her. Now she just has me."

Meri sat down on the pew and met Clarissa's eyes. "And sometimes, it is hard, no, to be the strong one," he asked, "and not just the little girl?"

She climbed up on the pew and sat down too, her feet dangling several inches off the floor. She looked at the crucifix hanging in the front of the church for a moment and finally turned toward Meri. "Are you an angel?" she asked.

Meri's smiled broadened and his laughter echoed in the empty cathedral. "No, tikna, an angel I am not," he said. "I am a traveler."

"Traveler?" she asked.

"Um, I am a gypsy," he said.

"Like the Hunchback of Notre Dame?" she asked with a smile.

He nodded. "Yes, like that."

"Is Mami a gypsy too?"

Meri smiled. "Yes, she is Drabarni, she sees things and tells us what to do," he explained.

"Like a mom?" Clarissa wondered.

Laughing, Meri reached over and patted Clarissa's head. "You are very wise," he said. "Yes, like a mom. She is the mother to our Rom family."

He picked up her backpack and handed it to her. "And now, tikna, it is time for us to walk to your home," he said. "It is night, but not too late. If we hurry, your mother will not know of your adventure."

She slipped the backpack over her shoulders and smiled up at him. "Thank you," she said. "I was very lost."

He nodded. "Come, I will show you the way."

They exited the church and walked together down the city street in the twilight. The streetlights glowed and most of the small Mom-and-Pop stores had "Closed" signs hanging from their doors. However, the taverns on the corners were open and the sounds and smells spilled onto the street. Clarissa was grateful Meri was walking with her.

"How did you come to be lost?" Meri asked.

She glanced up at him, then looked straight ahead. "It's a secret," she said. "I can't tell you."

He nodded slowly and they walked a little further. Pausing at a corner, they watched for cars and then quickly hurried to the other side. "Secrets can be heavy to carry," he said, after a few minutes had passed in silence. "Especially when you are so small. Can you not share a little with me?"

She looked up at him again, and then shook her head.

He watched a bus pass by and looked out into the distance. "Ah, well then, it must be an important secret."

She continued to walk, sighed and didn't respond. Her legs were aching and she was feeling cold again. All she wanted was to be home.

"And so, does your mother let you walk home from school alone?"

"No," she replied quickly. "She thinks Mrs. Gunderson is watching me."

Meri stopped walking for a moment and put his hand on her shoulder once again, turning her to face him. "Gunderson? She is *vaffadi mush*, a very bad person. Why does your mother allow this?"

Clarissa studied his face for a moment, he reminded her of her father when he was worried about something. She felt that she could trust him. "She doesn't know," she explained confidentially. "I don't tell her because she would worry."

"It is a parent's job to worry," he said. "It is not the child's job to worry."

He just doesn't understand, she thought. *Daddy and I took care of Mommy.*

"My mother is very sick," she finally said. "She is worried about so many things. I didn't want her to worry about me."

Meri rested his hand on her head. "But, *tikna*, you are the most important thing to worry about," he said. "She would not want you to be with a bad person."

"Well, I'm not anymore," she said. "So she doesn't have to worry."

She began walking again, looking everywhere but at Meri. He followed her, a few steps behind, amazed at the independence and courage of the little girl. He knew the neighborhood and he knew how Mrs. Gunderson and those like her acted, and he could probably guess what had happened. "So, they take your babysitting money and say you no tell your mother, or they hurt her, yes?"

Wide-eyed, Clarissa turned to him. "You can't say that to anyone," she cried, her eyes filling with tears. "They will kill my mother, they told me."

"I will tell no one," he promised, squatting down in front of her. "These are evil people and they will do as they say. You are right to be afraid. But you let them know you are under the protection of the Rom and they no longer will bother you."

"Why are they afraid of you?" she asked.

"Ah, because the gypsies have magic," he said with a grin. "And they no understand us, but they fear us."

"I'm not afraid of you," she said.

He laughed. "Because you have a shining soul," he said. "And Mami, she says angels do watch over you."

She nodded. "That must be my daddy," she explained matter-of-factly. "He's an angel now."

He reached out and stroked her cheek and nodded. "Yes, I am sure your daddy is watching over you too. Come now, we have one more stop before we go to your home."

A few blocks later they stopped at a playground Clarissa recognized. "I know this place," she said. "We are close to my house."

He nodded. "Yes, very close," he said. "But first, you learn your walk tomorrow."

Guiding her to the sandbox, he picked up a long stick. He drew a box in the sand. "This is your school," he said, drawing another long line perpendicular to the school. "And this is the road you must travel when you walk home. You know this road, yes? It is the road the bus travels on."

Then he drew various businesses she would recognize on her walk and which ones were safe places to go in and ask for help. "You are part of us now," he said. "And we are here to watch over you and help you. These places, the Rom are here. You tell them Mami is your friend and they will help you."

She nodded. "It doesn't seem so far, like this," she said.

"It is not far," he replied, "if you know the direction to take."

He pulled a paper bag out of his pocket. "And this, this is from Drina, my wife," he said. "Meat pies. Very good. One for you, one for your mother. You eat them for dinner."

She took the bag and smiled at him. "Thank you so much," she said. "And please say thank you to Drina for me."

Placing his arm around her shoulders, he walked the final two blocks to her apartment. At the front door they met Mrs. Gunderson and her nephew. Mrs. Gunderson's eyes widened when she saw Clarissa and Meri.

"Hello, Mrs. Gunderson," Clarissa said. "This is my friend, Meri. Mami Nadja sent him to help me walk home."

"I didn't know you were friends with Mami Nadja," she sputtered. "You never told me…"

Meri pulled Clarissa against him and met Mrs. Gunderson's eyes. "She is granddaughter to Nadja," he said. "She is under Rom protection. We are watching her."

Mrs. Gunderson's face turned pale. "Granddaughter?" she exclaimed. "She never told me. I didn't know."

"You now know," he said, his voice tight. "You now are warned."

Mrs. Gunderson reached into her shirt and pulled out the envelope Clarissa had given to her nephew that morning. "There was a mistake," she said, handing it to Clarissa. "This belongs to you. We don't want it."

"Her mother is protected too," Meri said.

"Nothing will happen to her," Mrs. Gunderson babbled, a bead of sweat appearing over her lip. "Please, believe me."

"You will not be bothering them again," he stated.

"But Clarissa, dear, you do want me to babysit you, don't you?"

Clarissa shook her head. "That's okay," she said. "I have angels watching over me."

Chapter Thirty-one

"Lydia, I'm so sorry," Mary said, as the group met in an antechamber near the courtroom. "I had no idea Thanner would lie to the jury about his brother."

Shaking her head, Lydia continued to pace along the front of the room. "There was nothing you could have done about it, Mary," she said. "We knew he would probably dig up the information about you and ghosts, and we played it the best way we could."

"We could have Gracie Williams testify," Bernie suggested. "She'd tell the jury that Mary wasn't nuts."

Lydia turned to Bernie. "Gracie Williams?" she asked.

"She's the psychologist who interviewed Mary after the shooting," Sean said. "She really didn't want to put Mary on disability, but at the time it was for the best."

Confused, Lydia turned to Mary. "What does he mean, at the time?"

"Well, I was pretty new to all this ghost stuff," Mary said. "And I really didn't know how to, let's say, filter very well. So everywhere I turned, I met a ghost. It was very hard to concentrate on my work as a police officer when there were ghosts from every era of Chicago's history popping up and trying to share their stories with me. It also spooked out a couple of my partners."

"So, your disability wasn't because...?" she began.

Mary grinned. "Because I was nuts?" she asked. "No, it was because I was distracted constantly, and it was a danger to the officers I was working with."

"As a matter of fact, Mary has been called in several times to work as a consultant on some cases," Sean said. "She has a great reputation and even the people who don't believe in the supernatural feel that she has an uncanny knack for getting good information."

"Do you think Gracie would be a good witness?" she asked.

Bernie and Sean looked at each other and started laughing. "Oh, yeah," Sean said. "She will be a great witness."

"But I'm not the one on trial," Mary said. "Why are we bringing in witnesses to testify on my behalf?"

"Because it's your word against Copper's," Lydia said. "And as it stands, Thanner is making it look like you invented the whole thing so Gary is blamed for Jeannine's death."

"But Copper lied about Jeannine at the hospital," Bradley said. "The jury heard that."

"And they also heard that Jeannine might have been running away from you," she said. "And if Thanner has Copper testify, you can bet that he will say he was protecting Jeannine from an abusive husband."

"All they need to win is reasonable doubt," Sean added. "If one juror thinks you might have been abusive, Copper walks."

"Well, that settles it," Mary said. "Call Gracie and tell her my psychiatric file is now an open book."

Chapter Thirty-two

"I hope his brother haunts him for the rest of his life," Rosie said, as they sat together in Mary's living room. "Imagine, lying in court."

She stood up and walked to the kitchen to refill her cup of tea.

Mary, sitting comfortably next to Bradley on the couch, nodded her agreement. "Well, I did make that suggestion to Garth," she admitted. "And he agreed that his brother needed a lesson in integrity. I'd love to be a fly on Thanner's bedroom wall tonight."

"What did you suggest?" Bradley asked.

"The usual," Mary said with a smile. "Groaning, moaning, some items being whipped across the room. Just a basic haunting, that's all."

"Brilliant," Ian said, lifting up his tea cup in a toast.

"That's my girl," Bradley said, hugging her and placing a kiss on the top of her head.

"So, what's next?" Stanley asked, leaning forward and snatching a cookie from the plate on the coffee table. "You need us to come and be character witnesses?"

"And you are quite a character, Stanley," Ian said, grabbing the final cookie before Stanley took it. "But I think I'd rather have you and Rosie testify for me. Who knows what's going to happen to me tomorrow on the stand."

Smiling, Mary shook her head. "You'll be fine, just wear the black shirt," she said. "There are plenty of women on the jury. However, Stanley, I will certainly keep you in mind, just in case. So, be ready to hop in your car and head to Sycamore."

"Anything to get me out of cleaning my office," he mumbled.

"I heard that Stanley," Rosie said, walking back into the room. "It's Tuesday and we get married on Friday. So, you don't have a lot of time left."

"That's right," Mary said. "There are only three days until your wedding. What can I do to help?"

Rosie sat down on a chair across from Mary. "Two things," she said. "We need to finish the project we started last night."

She lifted her eyebrow knowingly and Mary nodded. "Yes, that project," she agreed. "It does need to be finished before Friday."

"And, remember, we have a date at the spa on Thursday," Rosie reminded her. "Can you still make it?"

"Not only can I make it," she replied. "I am going to need a day of pampering after tomorrow's testimony. My whole life is going to be an open book; I only hope Lydia is able to keep the press out of the courtroom."

Ian leaned back in his chair and took the last bite of cookie. "If not, I'm sure there will be plenty of television opportunities in your future," he said. "Think of all the weird talk shows you'll be invited to be on."

Shaking her head, Mary laughed. "No thank you," she said. "I really don't want that kind of publicity."

"Come on now," Ian teased. "I thought that any publicity is good publicity, as long as they spell your name right."

Mary picked up a pillow and tossed it at him. "Thanks a lot!"

Ian tossed it back. "Anytime."

"How did your sleeping arrangements work last night?" Rosie asked.

Bradley cleared his throat a little. "Well, they were fine, just fine," he said.

"Iffen you don't mind sleeping with crazy rock and roll music," Stanley grumbled. "They had it playing to all hours of the morning."

"It was either that or not sleeping at all," Ian retorted. "Your snoring was loud enough to wake the dead."

Looking up at Bradley, Mary smiled. "And how did you sleep?"

"Like a baby," Bradley admitted. "Once I turned my music on, put my earplugs in and put my head under my pillow."

"You had earplugs?" Ian accused. "And you didn't share?"

Bradley shrugged. "Only one pair, sorry."

Ian stood up. "Well, if they worked, I think I'll swing by the store this evening before we call it a night," he said, turning to Stanley. "Anything you need while I'm there?"

"I wouldn't mind a quart of ice cream," he said. "Rocky Road. It helps me sleep."

Ian nodded. "Rocky Road it is. Bradley, anything I can pick up for you?"

"No, but I might tag along and get a couple things for breakfast," he said.

He turned and gave Mary a quick kiss. "Mind if we leave a little early?"

"No, actually, Rosie and I have a project we're working on," she explained. "And it wouldn't be a bad idea to get an early start."

"Stanley, do you want to come along?" Bradley asked. "Or do you just want the keys to my place?"

Stanley stood up and walked over to Rosie, giving her a kiss on the cheek. "I think I'll stop by my place afore the night gets too late," he said. "I'll pick up a couple of things for tomorrow. I'll meet you both later."

Ian nodded. "Okay, then, Rocky Road for you," he said. "Good night, ladies."

Chapter Thirty-three

Stanley entered his home cautiously. He only turned on the lamp in the living room, leaving the rest of the house in shadows. He had walked through the house so many times in the dark, he knew his way without light. He stopped in the middle of the living room, trying to read the atmosphere of the house. Even though he had seen a ghost, he didn't have a bad feeling when he entered his home. He felt a little uneasy, but he chalked that up to experiencing something new, rather than something evil.

"Verna," he called out softly. "I'm back. I've been trying for the life of me to remember what you want, I just can't."

He moved through the house, into the hall and finally into his bedroom. He turned on the bedside lamp, which cast a soft glow throughout the room. "Iffen it's so important, can you give me a clue somehow?" he asked. "I'm a little older than I was when we were last together. My memory wasn't great then, it's worse nowadays."

He opened his drawers and pulled out some clean clothing for the next couple of days and packed them inside an overnight case. "Maybe you're wondering why I'm sleeping at Bradley's," he muttered. "I guess I was spooked seeing you those first couple times. Guess it was easier to run away, than figure out what you wanted."

He put his bag on the floor and sat on the edge of the bed. "You know, I think you'd like Rosie," he said. "She's kind of a no-nonsense gal like you. She don't let me get away with much. She's even making me clean my office afore we get hitched on Friday."

Yawning, he stretched his arms and lay back on the bed, his feet still on the floor. "Don't know why I ain't sleeping here," he muttered. "I miss this old bed. It creaks like I do."

He grabbed a pillow from the top of the bed and stuffed it behind his head. "Maybe I'll just relax for a few minutes," he said. "They ain't gonna be done with their shopping for a while, anyways."

In a few moments, Stanley was asleep on the bed and snoring was filling the room. The streetlight cast a soft shadow through the curtains into the room, across the carpet, on the corner of the bed, on the bottom of the dresser and on the ghost standing next to the bed watching over the sleeping man.

Chapter Thirty-four

He was back in the hospital, he realized, as he walked down the halls that had become so familiar to him when Verna was sick. He knew the nurses by name, remembered each one of the paintings that hung on the wall and was familiar with the codes used by the operator to broadcast urgent information in a calm and friendly manner, so the residents and visitors weren't unduly alarmed.

Walking up the muted rose-colored hallways, he turned the corner at the nurse's station and walked to the left. Verna's room was 314. *Funny, he thought, even after so many years, I still remember her room number.*

The door was slightly ajar, as usual, because Verna didn't like being alone, especially as she got weaker. She wanted to be sure someone could hear her if she had to call for help. He slipped through the doorway and stood silently for a moment, watching his wife in her hospital bed. The pillow seemed too big for her head, her body too tiny and frail for the bed. The machines and tubes that surrounded her were more animated than she was. He cursed silently, she was shrinking away in front of his eyes and there was nothing he could do about it.

"Stanley," Verna called out weakly. "Is that you?"

He took a deep breath and pasted a smile on his face. "Hey, sweetheart, how are you doing this morning?" he asked as he strolled into the room.

He moved up to the side of the bed, took her tiny hand is his and leaned over and gave her a soft kiss. "I thought I'd steal you away from here and we could go on a picnic," he said.

She smiled up at him. "Oh, that would be lovely," she said, her voice thin and frail. "Where should we go?"

He stroked her hand gently. "Well, I was thinking we could drive up to Wisconsin," he suggested. "How about Devil's Lake? I could rent a boat and we could spend the afternoon paddling around under the trees."

"Then we could take a hike up on the bluffs," she added. "I love hiking on the bluffs."

He nodded and lifted her hand to his lips and kissed it. He willed back the tears that were threatening to spill into his eyes. "And we could watch the sunset from up there," he said. "I could bring your favorite picnic blanket in case it got cold."

She took a deep breath and sighed. "I do seem to get cold lately," she admitted. "I think my blood might have thinned down a mite."

"Well, you need to eat a little more and put some meat on your bones," he said, trying to be a little gruff because she would expect it. "You already got a cute, little girly figure, you don't need to get any thinner."

Laughing, she weakly pulled their clasped hands to her face and rested her cheek on them. "Do you really think I still have a cute girly figure?" she asked.

"Always," he agreed immediately.

Looking out into the room, she sighed. "Do you remember our first date?"

"Best day of my life," he said. "How could I forget?"

"You were so handsome in your uniform," she said. "My heart just fluttered at the sight of you."

"I saw you and my eyes popped out and my jaw dropped," he said. "I didn't know they let angels walk around on the earth."

There was silence between them for a few moments until finally she turned to him. "Stanley, I think this angel is going to be going up to heaven soon," she whispered.

He shook his head. "No," he whispered, his voice thick with emotion. "No, you're going to get better. We're going to have a lot of years ahead of us."

She loosened her hold on his hand and lifted it, so she could stroke his face. "I love you," she said with a gentle smile. "But we have to face reality."

He turned his face and kissed her hand urgently. "No, no we don't," he said, his voice breaking. "We hit harder times than this, and we've gotten through them, together. We'll get through this together too."

"It would be easier for me if you would just accept it," she said.

Shaking his head, tears flowing freely down his face, he whispered. "I don't want to make it easy. I want you to fight every step of the way."

"I've been fighting," she sighed. "And I'm so tired now. I'm just so tired."

He wiped his eyes and took a deep shuddering breath. "I know you have," he said, immediately contrite. "I'm sorry. I'm being selfish. I just...I just can't let you go."

"You're not letting me go," she said. "You're just saying goodbye for a little while. We'll be together again. But I want you to promise me something."

He nodded. "Anything."

She waited until he looked at her, met her eyes. She wanted to be sure she saw the promise in his eyes. "I want you to keep living," she said. "I want you to laugh again. I want you to hike at Devil's Lake without me. And I want you to fall in love again."

He shook his head. "No, I can't promise you that," he said. "You will be taking my heart with you. I've had enough love in my life. I don't..."

"Stanley," she interrupted, "I know you. You need a good woman by your side. Someone who will love you and take care of you and boss you around a little too."

"But..." he began.

"No buts," she said. "You can mourn for me, for a little while, but when the time is right, I want you to love again."

"I'll try," he said. "I promise I'll try."

She nodded. "That's enough. And I want you to tell her about me, show her the family photo album. I want to be friends with her when we meet someday. Promise?"

He nodded. "Yes, Verna, I promise. I'll tell her all about you."

She smiled and closed her eyes for a moment, her body exhausted. He watched her, his heart dropping, this couldn't be it. He wasn't ready to say goodbye. He leaned forward. "Verna?"

Her eyes opened slowly and she smiled softly. Then her eyes opened wider. "Oh, and one more thing," she said. "Don't forget…"

Then she wasn't saying words any longer, she was beeping, like his cell phone.

"Verna, what is it?" he said, the cell ringing over and over. "Tell me."

Stanley opened his eyes; the cell phone in his pocket was still ringing. He reached down and answered. "Hello," he said wearily.

"Stanley, it's Bradley. Are you okay? We've been waiting for you for about an hour."

Stanley looked at the clock on the nightstand. He'd been asleep for over an hour.

"Sorry, Bradley," he said. "Guess I fell asleep here at the house. I think I'll stay here tonight."

"Are you sure? We can come over…"

"No, I'm sure," he said. "I need to be here tonight. Good night."

"Good night Stanley."

Chapter Thirty-five

"Are you sure you want to do this tonight?" Mary asked as she and Rosie walked up steps to Rosie's home.

"Yes, I'm sure," she said with a decisive nod, gripping her keys tightly in her hand. "I'm actually surer than I was last night."

She turned to Mary with an excited smile. "We actually had him on the run last night," she said. "He was afraid of us."

"Yes, but tonight could be different," Mary warned. "Last night we had the element of surprise on our side. Tonight, he's probably expecting us."

Rosie paused before inserting the key into the lock. "Expecting us? What do you mean?"

Mary leaned on the wall, next to the door and met Rosie's eyes. "Last night we frightened him. He wasn't expecting us to act the way we did," she explained. "It seems that he is all about intimidation and fear. Tonight he won't have those weapons, at least not the way he's had them in the past. So, we don't know what's going to happen tonight."

"Do you want to go home, Mary?"

Mary shook her head. "I want to do whatever you want to do, Rosie. But I want you to understand this might not be a cakewalk."

Rosie looked down at the key in her hand. It would be so much easier to turn around and go back to the safety of Mary's house. Mary and Ian could come back to her house when she and Stanley were on their honeymoon and get rid of the ghosts. It would be so much easier to just walk away.

She thrust the key into the lock and shook her head. She'd done easier before, she'd run away before, she was not running away ever again. "Mary, I want to do this," she said, her determination evident in her eyes.

Nodding, Mary stood up and moved next to her. "Okay, then, let's do this."

The door opened quietly and the two women slipped inside. Rosie didn't bother turning on the light this time, there was enough filtered light from the streetlamps to see their way through the house. She walked directly to the bedroom, Mary hurrying behind her, and threw open the closet door.

"Okay, out with it," she yelled. "I'm not playing any games tonight."

Mary felt the atmosphere of the room change immediately and she pulled Rosie back a few steps. "Release the Kraken," Mary whispered ironically and waited to see just what was going to spew forth from the closet.

Darkness fell over the room, like a dark cloud had covered the little light available. The air became thicker and almost hard to breathe and it was charged with a tension that caused their hearts to race.

"Mary, what's happening?" Rosie whispered, clutching her friend's arm.

Mary took a deep breath and wrapped her arm around Rosie's waist. "I think we're about to find out."

Small tendrils of black slid from the inside of the closet and wrapped their way around the door frame and up the side of the walls. They sprouted more tendrils and pushed on throughout the wall. Soon the area was covered with a moving, squirming mass of darkness that continued to spread.

Rosie gasped and put her hand to her throat. "They're surrounding us," she said in a whispered panic. "They are going to wind themselves around us and strangle us to death."

Mary looked around the room, studying the moving mass. "Yeah, that could happen," she said casually. "But, really, they're kind of puny vines."

She took a step toward the wall.

"Stop!" Rosie screamed, grabbing her arm and pulling her back. "They'll kill you, Mary, they'll kill you."

"Rosie, they won't kill me," she said, turning back to her friend.

"Yes, they will," Rosie cried.

One look at her face convinced Mary that these vines represented something much more sinister to Rosie. Her eyes were wide with fear, her skin was pale and she was shaking. "Please Mary, I don't want you to die," she pleaded.

"Did you ever see these vines kill something, Rosie?" she asked, her voice calm.

Rosie nodded slowly and when she spoke, her voice seemed younger, like a child. "My kitty," she whispered, her eyes filling with tears as she looked around the room at the growing vines. "The kudzu killed my little kitty."

Mary put her hands on Rosie's shoulders and moved close enough to block her view of the room.

"Rosie, look at me," she said, "and pay attention."

Rosie's eyes snapped to attention. "Yes, ma'am," she responded politely.

"Who told you the vines killed your kitty?"

"Daddy," she said, her voice breaking. "I found my kitty in the backyard; it was stiff and cold and covered with kudzu. Daddy said the kudzu came out and grabbed my kitty and strangled the life out of it."

"What else did he tell you?" Mary asked, trying her best to keep the rage she felt toward Rosie's father to herself.

"He told me if I didn't do what he wanted, he would leave my closet door open and the kudzu would get in and kill me too," she said.

Mary remembered Rosie telling her about the abuse she suffered as a child and she realized it was far worse than she had thought.

"Rosie. Are you paying attention to me?" she asked.

Nodding, Rosie looked up into her face. Gone was the confident, self-assured woman and in her place was the child who had been manipulated by a sick, evil parent. Maybe she wasn't ready to face this yet. She looked around the room. The kudzu had now covered all of the furniture and most of the walls. Only the wall that held the doorway was clear. She took Rosie by the hand and led her from the room.

As if she had been in a dream, Rosie shook her head and looked around. "Mary, why aren't we in my bedroom?" she asked.

"Tell me about your kitten," Mary insisted gently.

"My kitten?" Rosie asked, a little confused.

"The kitten that died in the kudzu."

"Oh, that kitten," Rosie said sadly. "I haven't thought about her in years."

"You need to think about her now," Mary said. "You need to remember as much as you can about that time in your life."

Rosie nodded, then closed her eyes and thought about it for a moment. "My mother and I had gone away for a few days," she said, biting her lip as she tried to remember all the details. "My mother was hurt, her face was bruised. She must have fallen…"

Looking up at Mary, Rosie shook her head. "He hit her," she said, as she finally realized what had happened to her mother. "He beat my mother. She didn't fall down. Ever. He beat her."

Mary nodded. "Yes, he probably did," she agreed. "Men like your father are bullies and like to pick on people and animals who are weaker than they are. It gives them a perverted sense of power."

"My kitten," she said slowly. "He must have killed my kitten."

"He might have been angry that you and your mother left," Mary suggested.

She walked back to the open bedroom door and looked at the kudzu on the walls. "And he left her in the yard. He didn't even bury her," she said. "He left her there so I would find her."

Mary followed her. "He wanted you to be afraid, Rosie," she said. "His greatest power is fear."

She shook her head and walked into the room, to the vines on the wall. "You know, if you think about it, the kudzu only tried to give my kitten a proper burial," she said. "Another couple of days and I would have never found her."

She reached forward and pulled a vine from the wall. It writhed in her hand, but she kept a tight hold on it. "It can't hurt me," she said, grasping it with both hands and ripping it in half. "It's just a damn plant."

The black vine melted into thin air and the kudzu on the walls began to recede back into the closet.

"Who else hid in your closet, Rosie?" Mary asked.

Her head snapped up and she turned and stared at her friend. "Oh, you're right. Mary, how could I forget that?" she asked, bewildered.

"Our minds are wonderful instruments; they try to protect us from the things that frightened us. They often hide the things we can't handle," she said, she put her hand on Rosie's shoulder. "But you can handle this now."

Nodding, Rosie walked over and stood in front of her closet. She took a deep breath. "Daddy, come out of the closet," she yelled. "Dammit, you come out of that closet right now!"

The darkness seemed to deepen and the door actually shook.

"Remember, he wins when you're afraid," Mary whispered, coming up and standing behind her back. "Don't show your fear, Rosie."

The ghost was tall and almost spider-like as he crept out of the closet. Darkness encompassed him and there was little left of his human form. His eyes glowed red and his teeth were sharp and pointed. He crawled toward Rosie. "What do you want, little girl?" he hissed, like a reptilian creature, his voice was slow and cold.

Rosie looked over her shoulder, a frightened question on her face.

"Tell him what you want," Mary said, nodding her encouragement. "Tell him exactly what you want."

Rosie faced the creature, which was now looming over her. "I want you to leave me alone," she said slowly. "I want you out of my life."

"You don't mean that," he replied. "You have always loved me. You told me so."

She swallowed. Her heart was pounding against her chest and the little girl inside wanted to dart under the covers. She could run, but she realized she would be running forever. This time, this once, she had to take a stand.

"I didn't love you," she whispered, her mouth dry.

"You're lying to me girl," he spit. "You know what happens when you lie."

She nearly flinched, nearly gave him the satisfaction. Then she turned and saw herself reflected in the mirror over her dresser. She saw the photos of the people who really loved her. Who taught her what love was all about.

Instead of stepping back, she stepped forward and the ghost flinched. Rosie felt a surge a power. "I hated you," she cried, releasing all of the feelings she had bottled up inside. "I hated how you treated me and my mother. Every night I prayed that you would die. You are evil, selfish and you are a coward."

"You wanted me," he insisted. "I was giving you what you wanted."

"No, you weren't, and you knew that," she said sadly. "But you can't hurt me any longer. I am not afraid of you. I am stronger than you are. I can't be manipulated any longer. You need to leave."

Mary noticed his size was diminished by Rosie's words. "Tell him again," she encouraged.

"Go away," Rosie said. "Never come back. You are not welcome here, you are not wanted here. Your body died a long time ago. But you were dead to me much, much earlier than that."

"You need me," he said, as he shrunk back into the closet.

Rosie shook her head. "No, I never needed you," she said. "I needed a father who would protect me and that was never you."

"You are afraid of me," he said, his voice thin and weak.

She took hold of the closet door and laughed bitterly. "No, I'm not," she said, and then realized what she was saying was true.

Wonderment spread across her face. "No, I'm not. I'm not."

She watched him shrink away and disappear into the shadows of the closet. Closing the closet door firmly, she laid her head against it and took a deep breath.

Mary walked over to her and placed her hand on Rosie's shoulder. "You did it," she said. "He's gone and he's never coming back."

Rosie turned so Mary could see the tears forming in her eyes. "Why am I sad?" she wept. "I really did hate him."

Mary wrapped her arms around her friend. "You're just sad for what could have been, what should have been," she said. "Fathers are supposed to protect their daughters. They are supposed to be our heroes. The ones we can turn to when things get bad. You never had that and the little girl in you is mourning for the loss."

Rosie wiped a hand over her eyes and nodded. "But I have friends who I can turn to."

"Always," Mary said, leading her friend out of the room. "Always."

Rosie sniffed and leaned her head on Mary's shoulder.

"You know what I need?" she asked. "What I really need?"

"Yeah, chocolate," Mary replied. "Come on, my treat."

Chapter Thirty-six

"The court would like to call Dr. Gracie Williams to the stand," the clerk stated.

The statuesque mahogany-colored woman stood slowly and glanced through lowered eyelashes at the clerk before making her way to the stand. He cleared his throat and loosened his neck collar before he approached her with the Bible.

"Do you...?" he began, but his voice came out in a high-pitched squeak.

He cleared his throat and held the Bible out. Gracie softly stroked the book with her fingertips before resting her hand on top of it.

"Do you swear to tell the truth, the whole truth and nothing but the truth, so help you God?" he asked.

She nodded and smiled at him. "Well, of course I do, sugar."

He cleared his throat once more. "Thank you," he replied. "You may be seated."

She sat gracefully, her legs crossed at the knee and her hands folded modestly in her lap. She watched and waited, like a sleek tiger, for the attorney to approach.

Lydia came forward. "Ms. Williams..."

"That's Dr. Williams," she interrupted softly. "But you can call me Gracie."

Lydia nodded. "Thank you, Gracie. Can you state your occupation for the jury?"

"Certainly, I'm a psychologist and I work for the Chicago Police Department."

"And what is involved in your kind of work for the Department?"

"Well, it just depends on the day," she said with a smile. "I could be working up a criminal profile on a serial killer, I could be counseling police officers or I could be performing psychiatric evaluations for the Department."

"I'd like to focus on psychiatric evaluations," Lydia said.

"I thought you might," Gracie replied.

"You evaluated Mary O'Reilly after she was shot," Lydia stated.

"Honey, I evaluated Mary O'Reilly when she was first hired, every time she was up for promotion and after she was shot," Gracie said. "What would you like to know?"

"In your professional opinion, is Mary O'Reilly delusional?" Lydia asked.

Gracie's loud laughter echoed in the courtroom. She looked at Mary, and they shared a wide smile. "I'm sorry, do you mean, you want to know if she's nuts, in my professional opinion?"

Lydia looked slightly uncomfortable.

"I'm sorry, sweetie," Gracie added. "My bedside manner can be a little off-putting."

She turned to the jury. "Let me tell you a little about Mary O'Reilly," she said, adjusting herself on

229

the seat so she was turned in their direction. "I met Mary O'Reilly when she was a cadet in the Police Academy. She had just graduated with honors from college and could have easily gone on to law school. She had the brains and she was offered a scholarship. I remember the first thing I said to her, 'Girl, are you nuts?'"

Gracie laughed at her own joke and the jury laughed along.

Sitting in the audience, Mary was able to smile at her friend, remembering the moment. The knots in her stomach loosening a little. *Gracie is going to be an amazing witness*, she thought. *We are not going to lose this case because of me.*

Bradley reached over, took Mary's hand and squeezed it. "How are you doing?" he whispered.

She nodded slightly, trying to look positive. "I'm good," she said.

Please don't hate me if we lose this case, she pleaded silently.

He slid over on the bench, so he was pressed against her side. He leaned over, so his lips were next to her ear. "Without you we wouldn't be here in this courtroom. Without you I would not know the truth about Jeannine and Clarissa. Without you we wouldn't have had the chance to prosecute Copper," he whispered. "And without you my life would be empty."

She turned her head and met his eyes. "I just wanted…" she began.

He gently put his finger on her lips. "I know, you wanted to fix everything," he said with a wry smile. "But even you, Mary O'Reilly, are not responsible for how things turn out. Okay?"

She took a deep breath and nodded. "Okay."

"Now enjoy Gracie's testimony, because she's good," Bradley said, a twinkle in his eye.

A real smile appeared on Mary's face. "Yes. Yes, she is."

Gracie was continuing her testimony. "It was then I started to understand what made Mary tick. She explained that all she had ever wanted to do was become a police officer, like her dad, her granddad and her great-granddad. She told me it was an O'Reilly tradition. She wanted to risk her life to protect the people of Chicago. I told her she could have had more money, more prestige and a better wardrobe," Gracie said, shaking her head. "But no, this was a calling."

She lifted her hand and placed it on her chest. "She was a police officer in her heart."

Leaning forward, she placed her hands on the ledge in front of her. "I interviewed Mary every couple of years or so, it's mandatory for the Department," she continued. "I'd never met a more well-adjusted, good-hearted person than Mary. She was the first to volunteer and the last to toot her own horn. We could use several dozen more like her."

"What happened after she was shot?" Lydia prompted.

Gracie turned and nodded at Lydia. "What happened at the Department? We all were in shock. We walked through the halls, passing each other, tears in our eyes, not saying a word. But we were all praying, I can promise you that. We were all praying for her."

Bradley interlocked his fingers with Mary's and held her hand in his.

Gracie wiped away a little moisture from her eye and took a deep breath. "Unless you work on the force, with the force, you don't really understand. We're family...because we have to be. We've got each other's backs and without that, we're dead, literally. We know each other's problems, from spouses to kids to money to the heartbreak of psoriasis. And Mary, well, she was everyone's kid sister."

Sitting back in her chair, she paused for a moment and you could see that she was struggling to maintain her composure. "When...when we heard that she had pulled through," she paused again, blotting her eyes with a lacy handkerchief, "we just cried. From the biggest, toughest, meanest cop on the force to the ladies in the records department. And we weren't ashamed of our tears. We felt like we had witnessed a miracle, because of the cops that had been on the scene. Cops that know. They didn't hold out much hope for Mary."

"And after she recovered from her surgery?" Lydia prompted. "What happened then?"

"Mary came to me before I had the chance to even set up an appointment," Gracie said. "She told me she needed to talk with me. Said that something happened to her when she was in surgery."

She paused and let her gaze travel through the courtroom and rest on Mary. She smiled at her and nodded. "Now, let me tell you," Gracie said. "Mary did not have to come to me. She didn't have to report what happened to her. She could have gone on her way and passed any evaluation I had given to her. But that's not Mary. She wanted to be sure that nothing in her new-found talent would disrupt her abilities or distract her from doing her job."

She turned back to the jury. "I've done a lot of reading on near-death experiences," she said. "And what Mary describes is pretty much casebook. But then her story takes a slight detour. She's given a choice. She could have gone on. All of those other folks in the cases I've read, they wanted to go on, wanted to go to the light, but they were turned away. Mary was given a choice and, because of her love for her family and her sense of duty, she came back. And when she came back, she had an extra sense."

Gracie sat back and folded her arms across her chest. "Now, people could say, 'She must be nuts, she thinks she sees ghosts,' and I can tell you, I put her through a battery of tests and she passed every one with flying colors. I can also tell you that there is a lot of conversation in the field of psychology about parapsychology, or the study of psychic phenomenon. The only reason we doubt some of the information received through 'psychic' methods is because it was obtained or occurred through a mechanism that is currently unknown to the scientific world."

She paused for a moment. "Fifty years ago, if I told you I wanted to put a large needle into the belly of a pregnant woman and extract some amniotic fluid, and with that fluid I could predict the illnesses the unborn baby would have when he was eighty years old, you would probably think I was nuts. But now, through DNA testing, we can spot genetic markers that show the potential risks for mental illness, autism and epilepsy not to mention hundreds of other rare or genetic diseases and disabilities."

"Just because we don't understand something now, doesn't mean it's not true," she concluded.

"Thank you, Gracie," Lydia said. "No further questions."

"Would the defending counsel…" the judge began.

"Yes, we would, your honor," Greg Thanner interrupted, making his way toward the witness stand.

"You seem fond of Ms. O'Reilly," he said to Gracie.

Gracie nodded. "Yes, I am," she replied, her voice was now tight and she looked down her nose at the man.

"Would that fondness encourage you to gloss over some aspects of her mental health?"

Gracie sat up straight and glared at the man. "I'm sorry, but did you just accuse me of perjury?"

He shook his head. "No, I…"

"Because I don't lie in court," she continued. "I tell the truth. Even if it's uncomfortable. Even if it might lose the court case. Even if it's unbelievable. Because I believe in this system of justice."

Then she leaned forward and met his eyes. "And how about you? Do you ever lie in court?"

"I am not the one on the witness stand," he said, stepping back.

"And you didn't answer my question," she responded.

"Objection," he cried, turning to the judge. "The witness is not supposed to be questioning the defense."

"Sustained," the judge said, a smile passing over her features. "However, I would suggest the defense not accuse the witness of perjury."

He turned back to Gracie. "Do you believe Mary O'Reilly to be an honest person?" he asked.

"Honey, weren't you listening to the first part of my testimony at all?" Gracie asked. "Don't be wasting my time here on the stand. I said she was honest, loyal, brave, and all those other things the Boy Scouts are. This girl is true blue."

"Ms. Williams…" he began.

"That would be Dr. Williams," she interrupted.

"Gracie," he began again.

"No, honey, that would be Dr. Williams," she repeated.

"You don't like me, do you?"

"Honey, I don't know you," she replied. "And if you're trying to pick me up, well, let me clue you in. You ain't my type."

Thanner's face turned red and he glared at Gracie. "Dr. Williams, is there any way to verify that Ms. O'Reilly is telling the truth?"

"Sure there is, give her a lie detector test," she replied.

"Why didn't the Police Department give her a lie detector test before they allowed her to have access to disability?" Thanner asked. "Don't you think it would be been wise to see if she was lying about her...ability?"

Gracie leaned forward. "Well, if you had done your homework and read those little reports you have in your hand," she said, "you would see that we did give her a lie detector test. And you would also see that she passed the test with flying colors. She's not lying about her ability to see ghosts."

"Do you believe in ghosts, Dr. Williams?" Thanner asked, his face twisted with scorn.

"Mr. Thanner, I believe in God," she said pointedly. "And I believe in angels. I believe in things I can't see, like faith and love. Why not ghosts? Why wouldn't those who have gone on before us get a chance to visit again?"

"You didn't answer my question," he countered.

"Yes, Mr. Thanner, I believe in ghosts," she said.

"No further questions, your honor," Thanner said.

Gracie stood and took a moment to smile at the jury before she walked across the courtroom, like a model on a catwalk. She paused for a moment at Mary's row. "He's a hunk," she said, nodding toward Bradley. "I'd keep hold of him if I were you."

Mary grinned at her. "Oh, I intend to," she replied.

"That's my girl," Gracie said. "You take care now."

She left the room, the sound of her high heels echoing down the hall.

Chapter Thirty-seven

"It's too bad Gracie couldn't join us for lunch," Mary said, as they sat down together at a small restaurant not far from the courthouse. "I really wanted to thank her for her testimony."

The waitress came over, handed them menus and quickly took their beverage orders.

"Well, I, for one am glad she didn't stay," Sean said. "That defense attorney made chopped liver out of my testimony. Either it was entrapment or a conspiracy against Copper. I hope the jury didn't buy it."

Ian slapped his menu down on the table. "If this case were tried under English Common Law, we wouldn't be having this discussion," he said. "Copper would be well and good behind bars already."

"Well, there is that small matter of the war we won," Sean said, "where we got in our boats and waved 'bye-bye' to English Law."

"And a lot of good that's done you," Ian gumbled.

Bradley looked over the top of his menu at Ian. "So, you think your testimony would have been more accepted in a British Court of Law?" he asked. "Would they have accepted Jeannine's testimony through Mary?"

Sighing, Ian shook his head. "No, they would have laughed their bloody wigs off," he said. "This is so frustrating. I have no idea what the jury is going to do."

"Well, at least it isn't all going his way," Mary said.

"How do you know that?" Bradley asked.

"Lydia told me that Thanner is going to have Copper testify this afternoon," she explained. "If this were a slam dunk, there is no way he'd risk Copper saying something stupid."

"Like, hey folks, I'm a murderer and a rapist and a fairly poor dentist too," Ian suggested.

"Could you hypnotize him and get him to say that?" Sean asked.

The waitress came back, interrupting their conversation, and took their order.

"Do you think the defense has any other witnesses?" Sean asked.

Mary shook her head. "Lydia said we would be wrapping things up this afternoon, so I think Copper is the only witness on the docket."

"And then we wait?" Ian asked.

Bradley nodded. "Yes, and then we wait."

Chapter Thirty-eight

"The court would like to call Dr. Gary Copper to the stand," the clerk said.

Gary Copper stood and slowly made his way around the defense table and to the witness stand. He stepped up to the stand, faced the clerk and put his hand on the Bible.

"Do you swear to tell the truth, the whole truth and nothing but the truth, so help you God?" the clerk asked.

He nodded and said, "Yes."

"He's lying," Ian whispered to Mary, sitting next to him.

"How can you tell?" she asked quietly.

"His mouth is open," Ian replied.

The defense attorney followed his client to the front of the courtroom and stood facing him. "Dr. Copper, can you please tell the jury about your relationship with Jeannine Alden?" he asked calmly, smiling over his shoulder at the jury.

"My wife and I had been good friends with Jeannine and Bradley," he explained. "They invited us over for dinner and then we invited them. You know, the way friends treat each other. My wife and I often commented how nice it was to find a couple that we both got along with. But, after my wife left me, things got a little distant. They were still friendly, but I'm sure it was harder to invite me, a single man over to their home. However, because Bradley had such erratic hours, whenever there was a mechanical issue at their house, Jeannine would call me to help."

He sat back and smiled at the jury. "We became the best of friends," he said. "She would listen to my venting about my wife and, eventually, she opened up about her relationship with Bradley."

Turning to Thanner, he leaned forward. "Should I tell them about the abuse?" he asked.

Bradley, sitting between Mary and Sean, jumped forward in his seat. Both Mary and Sean placed a restraining hand on his arms. "Don't react," Sean whispered, "you'd be playing right into his game."

Grudgingly, Bradley sat back and tried to keep his face emotionless.

"Yes, Dr. Copper, do tell us about the abuse," Thanner said.

"Objection, your honor," Lydia called out. "There is absolutely no evidence of abuse of any kind, from any other viable source. Mr. Thanner is allowing his witness and his client to spin fantasies for the jury."

The judge looked down on Thanner. "Do you have any other witnesses that can testify and verify your client's claim of abuse?" the judge asked.

Thanner shook his head. "No, your honor, but…"

The judge's gavel struck solidly. "Sustained. There will be no talk of abuse," the judge interrupted.

Thanner scowled and walked back to Copper. "Dr. Copper, what happened on the day the Alden's home was broken into?" Thanner asked.

"I was home, getting ready for work," he said, "when there was a knock on my back door. I answered it to find Jeannine standing on the deck, with an overnight bag in her hand. She asked me if she could come in and, of course, I said yes."

"Of course he did," Ian muttered, "the bloody liar."

"She explained to me that she was leaving Bradley," Copper continued. "She wasn't sure where she was going to go. I could see she was upset but she didn't tell me about the break-in. She stayed with me for several hours and then I lent her some money so she could get out of Sycamore."

"So you gave Jeannine Alden money and then she left your home?" Thanner said.

"Yes, I didn't see Jeannine until a few days before her baby was born," he explained. "She showed up late one afternoon at my office. I could tell she was under the influence of some kind of drug. I was worried about her and the baby."

"Why didn't you call her husband?" Thanner asked.

"She begged me not to call," he said. "She was worried he would hurt her and their unborn child."

Mary held on to Bradley's hand with both of her hands. She felt his grip tighten as Copper's lies continued. "Lydia will tear him up," she whispered.

"So, Dr. Copper, what did you do?" he asked.

"I have a small apartment below my offices," he said. "I offered her the use of it, until her baby came. I thought it would be okay for her to stay there. But on the night her baby was born, she called me, screaming. She was in labor. I rushed over to find that she had taken some of the drugs I had in the office. I was going to drive her to the closest hospital, but she insisted that we go somewhere she could be anonymous. So, I headed out on Highway 88 and drove into Chicago."

"Why did you falsify her records?"

"She begged me not to let them know her name," he said. "I had no idea she had a drug allergy. I just was trying to help her."

"And why did you bury her under your wife's name?"

"When we were driving into the hospital, she made me promise that if anything were to happen to her, I would protect her child," he said. "Keep the baby away from Bradley. This was the only way I could accomplish her last wish."

"Did you love Jeannine Alden?" Thanner asked.

Copper shook his head. "No, she was just a person in need, that's all."

Thanner nodded. "Thank you, Dr. Copper," he said. "No further questions."

The judge turned to Lydia. "Would you like to cross examine the witness?" she asked.

Lydia nodded. "Oh yes, your honor."

Lydia walked forward, but didn't get too close to the witness stand. The guy made her skin crawl. "Dr. Copper," she said. "Isn't it true that Jeannine had parents in Sycamore? Parents that were very close to her and parents who financially could have supported her in any way she needed?"

He shrugged. "I never met her parents."

"Yet, you ask us to believe that a woman, who from all accounts of neighbors, coworkers and family members, had a very happy marriage, suddenly showed up on your doorstep after her house had been ransacked, and asked you for help?"

"Yes, that's what happened," he insisted.

"And why didn't she go to her parents?" she asked.

He paused for a moment. "Because they insisted she stay with her husband," he said. "She told me they wanted her to remain in her unhappy marriage."

"Well, that's interesting, Dr. Copper, because neither of Jeannine's parents had any kind of conversation with her about her marriage being unhappy," she said. "Both of them testified that they had just seen Jeannine a day before her disappearance. They remember her being thrilled with her pregnancy and being very much in love with her husband."

"Well, I only know what she told me," he said. "I don't know why she would lie to her parents; she must have had her reasons."

"Dr. Copper, do you have a record or receipt of the money you gave Jeannine Alden?" she asked. "Perhaps a withdrawal slip from the day she came to you?"

He shook his head. "No, I, um..." he paused. "I just gave her some cash on hand."

"You had enough cash on hand to have allowed Jeannine to live away from all of her friends and family for a number of months until the baby was born?" she asked. "How much money was that, exactly?"

Copper stared over at Thanner for a moment and then faced Lydia. "I don't recall," he said. "It was eight years ago."

"And yet you seem to recall all the other parts of her disappearance with no problem," Lydia said. "I would think that you had to have given her a sizable amount of cash."

"Well, money doesn't matter when you are helping a friend," he replied.

"So you testified," Lydia responded. "When Bradley Alden was going to lose his home, you gave him the money to save it. I find that odd, Dr. Copper, considering you testified that he abused his wife and she felt unsafe coming back to this community because he was there. Why would you save his home? One would think you would want Bradley out of the neighborhood, so Jeannine could return."

"Well, it was after she was dead," he said. "So there was nothing to worry about anymore."

"That's right, after she was dead," Lydia said.

"Dr. Copper, what gave you the idea to put your wife's name for Jeannine on the death certificate?"

He smiled and paused for a moment. "Well, I figured she wasn't going to be using it."

"Why didn't you think she'd ever use it?"

He shook his head. "You can't use that," he said.

"I'm sorry, Dr. Copper, I can't use what?"

"You can't use the fact the police found my wife's body in a freezer in my home for evidence," he said. "It was unlawful entry, they had no search warrant."

"Dr. Copper, I didn't say a word about your wife," Lydia said. "But you just admitted that your wife's body was in a freezer in your basement. Would you like to tell the jury about that?"

Copper turned frantically to the judge. "But I thought…Thanner said they couldn't use it in court," he stammered.

"The prosecuting attorney was not allowed to use the evidence found by the police department during their unlawful search," the judge explained. "However, she can certainly follow up on information you just divulged on the stand. Please answer the question, Dr. Copper."

Sweat started to bead on his forehead and upper lip. "I…um…" he began, looking frantically at his attorney.

Lydia moved over, blocking his attorney from his view. "Your wife, Dr. Copper," she said. "I'm sure the jury would like to know how she came to be residing in a freezer in your basement."

"We had an argument," he said. "We were standing at the top of the stairs and she was angry with me. She stepped backward, without realizing how close she was to the top of the stairs, and she fell."

"If it was an accident, why didn't you call the paramedics or the police?" she asked.

"I ran down the stairs after her," he said. "And I could see her neck was broken and she was dead. I realized our baby was inside her, dying too. So, I decided to perform a C-section on her and get the baby out."

"You didn't call 911," Lydia reiterated. "You decided to perform an operation on the floor of your hallway."

"There wasn't time," he said. "The baby only had a few minutes before it died."

"What happened?"

He shook his head, tears falling down his face. "The baby died. Our baby died," he said. "She killed our baby. Her selfish decision to leave me killed our baby."

"And how did her body and the body of your child end up in the freezer?" Lydia asked.

Glancing over at the jury, he could see the horror on their faces. He wiped the tears from his face and tried to regain his composure. "There was so much blood on the floor," he said. "And now there were knives and my fingerprints involved, I was worried the police would think I killed her."

"But a coroner would have been able to prove the initial cause of death," Lydia countered, "if it indeed was from a fall."

He leaned forward in the witness stand, his face contorted in rage. "I didn't kill my wife," he yelled. "She fell. I didn't kill her."

Lydia walked over to the prosecutor's table and picked up a folder. "I would like to introduce this report into evidence," she told the judge. "Unless the defendant introduced the death of his wife, we didn't think we could use it. But this is a coroner's report on the remains of Beverly Copper, Gary Copper's wife."

She laid the report on the judge's desk and turned to the jury. "The coroner did not find any evidence of a broken neck. Even though Dr. Copper had dismembered his wife, wrapped her in plastic and stored her in an upright freezer, he kept her trunk and skull in place. The coroner believes the cause of death was exsanguination caused by severing of the aorta."

She turned to Copper. "Your wife died because she bled to death," she said. "You performed your operation on a woman who was still alive and you cut through her aorta. You killed your wife, Dr. Copper."

Chapter Thirty-nine

"Clarissa, I'm home," Becca called as she entered the apartment.

She leaned against the wall and tried to catch her breath. It had taken her five minutes to walk up the stairs, having to pause every few steps to catch her breath. She wiped the perspiration off her forehead and took a deep shuddering breath.

Clarissa came running from the kitchen with a wide smile on her face. "I have a special dinner for us," she said. "Meat pies! And they smell delicious."

Becca shook her head. "Meat pies? Mrs. Gunderson shouldn't have done that," she said. "I barely pay her enough to take care of you. She doesn't need to make us food."

Clarissa's stomach nearly turned at the thought of any food from Mrs. Gunderson's house, but she didn't want to talk about Mrs. Gunderson, so she just smiled. "Just smell them, Mommy," she said. "Don't they smell the bestest? I got them yesterday, but you were too tired when you got home from work. So I saved them for today."

Lifting the flaky pie to her nose, Becca inhaled and had to agree that the scent was heavenly. Her stomach rumbled and she quickly put her hand on her abdomen. "Oh, my, I must be hungry," she said.

She lifted her fork and cut into the pie. Thick brown gravy oozed out and coated the crust. Becca could see large chunks of vegetables and meat. She brought a forkful to her mouth and took a large bite. The buttery flavor of the crust combined perfectly with the spicy gravy and meat combination. She quickly scooped up another piece.

"This is wonderful," she said to Clarissa, who was also enjoying her meal.

Looking up, brown gravy on her chin, Clarissa smiled. "It's even better than restaurant food."

"Yes, you're right," Becca agreed, "it really is."

The conversation halted and they both concentrated on their food. Finally, their plates wiped clean, Becca sat back and sighed. "That was so delicious. I need to go up to Mrs. Gunderson and thank her."

"No, that's okay, Mommy," Clarissa said. "I already said thank you to her."

"Well, I appreciate that," her mother replied. "But I think it's necessary for me to thank her. She is really doing so much for our family. I need to let her know how much I appreciate her."

Clarissa looked down at her lap for a moment and, with a sigh, lifted her head and met her mother's eyes. "Mrs. Gunderson didn't make the meat pies," she said.

"Clarissa, where did they come from?" her mother asked.

"Meri's wife, Drina, made them for us."

"Meri? Drina? Who are they?"

"They're gypsies, just like the Hunchback of Notre Dame," she explained. "And they are friends of Mami Nadja at the nursing home."

"Mami Nadja? The woman at the nursing home who knew I'd been taking drugs from them?" she asked, her voice raising and her breathing becoming a little erratic.

"Mommy, it's okay," Clarissa said, sliding out of her chair and running around the table to hug her mother. "They are our friends. They want to protect us."

Becca put her hand on Clarissa's head and stroked her hair gently. "Darling, you don't understand," she said. "We can't trust anyone. The bad man who wants to find us has money and money can make good people do bad things."

"No, Mommy, Meri won't do bad things," she said.

Becca sighed. "Perhaps he won't," she said. "But he might not understand that it is bad. He might just tell someone where a little girl named Clarissa lives. He might accidentally give our secret away. I can't risk it. Please try to understand, Clarissa."

She wrapped Clarissa in her arms and held her. "I can't let them get you, sweetheart," she whispered into her hair. "I can't let anything happen to you."

Sighing, Clarissa nodded. "I won't talk to Meri anymore," she said sadly. "I promise."

251

Becca placed her hands on Clarissa's shoulders and gently moved her out of the embrace, so she could see her face. She knew Clarissa would be disappointed, but she needed to be honest with her daughter. "Darling, you won't ever see Meri again because we are going to have to move," she explained. "It's not safe here anymore."

"But where will we go?" Clarissa asked.

Becca pushed herself out of her chair and leaned against the table. "Let me count my tips," she said, "and see how much money we have. Then I'll be able to decide."

Clarissa watched her mother struggle down the hallway into the living room. She heard the sound of Becca's purse being emptied as coins jingled against the surface of the table. She didn't want to leave. She liked Meri. She wanted to be part of the gypsy people. She wanted to be protected from people like Mrs. Gunderson and her nephew.

Then she remembered the look of worry on her mother's face and she knew what she had to do. She picked up her backpack, reached inside and withdrew the envelope.

Becca divided the coins into piles of quarters, dimes, nickels and pennies. Then she created stacks to make the tally easier. She started with the quarters and was relieved to find the stacks totaled twenty dollars. Now to count the dimes.

She heard Clarissa enter the room, but was concentrating on keeping the total in her head, so she didn't pay attention to her until she saw the crumpled envelope slide toward her on the table.

"What's this?" she asked.

"It's the babysitting money," Clarissa said. "Mrs. Gunderson gave it back to me today."

"But…I don't understand," Becca replied. "Why would she do that?"

"She said there was a mistake," Clarissa said. "She said it was ours and she didn't want it."

Becca took the envelope and opened it, noting the bundle of dollar bills still clipped together. "Clarissa, this means we can go far away," she said, a smile spreading on her face. "We can get bus tickets to Florida or Georgia. We can go somewhere no one can ever find us."

Chapter Forty

Mary and Rosie, wrapped in large towels, sat on the back row in the sauna, inhaling the eucalyptus-scented steam. Mary leaned her head back against the wall and relaxed. "Rosie, this was an amazing idea," she said. "I feel so relaxed."

"Well, after what we've been through lately, I thought we both deserved a spa day," she said. "Besides, I want to look my best tomorrow night."

Mary smiled. "Poor Stanley won't know what hit him."

Rosie giggled. "I'm all about shock and awe," she said. "I'm thinking about getting a little heart tattoo on my nether regions, what do you think?"

Choking, Mary sat up and turned to her friend. "You are not…"

"I don't know," Rosie said with a grin. "Stanley might like it."

"Well, if it's for Stanley, you ought to be getting a slice of pie tattoo," Mary teased.

Rosie turned and looked over her shoulder. "Does this banana cream make my butt look fat?" she replied.

They both laughed and Mary resumed her relaxed state against the wall. "I am so happy for you, Rosie," she said. "I think you and Stanley are going to be so happy together."

Rosie leaned back too and nodded. "Underneath all of those grumbles, he really is a charming man," she said.

"And he adores you," Mary said. "It's always wonderful when a man adores his wife."

"Just like Bradley adores you," Rosie added.

Mary grinned. "Yeah, he does, doesn't he?" she said. "I am so lucky."

"Well, I think he's lucky too," Rosie added.

"And I think Stanley's lucky," Mary said.

"Well, he will be tomorrow night," Rosie laughed.

"Rosie!" Mary said, her face turning red. "I can't believe you just said that!"

Blotting away some of the perspiration with a thick face towel, Rosie turned to her friend. "Mary, there is nothing embarrassing about sex," she said. "It's the most beautiful, natural and fulfilling part of a relationship."

"I have to admit, I'm a little worried about the whole wedding night thing," Mary said. "I don't want to do anything wrong."

A gurgling laugh escaped Rosie's lips. "Oh, sweetheart, there is no way you could do anything wrong," she said. "The secret is..."

"What?" Mary asked, leaning closer.

She met Mary's eyes. "The secret is to relax, communicate and enjoy. Don't worry about performing or expectations. Sex is a bond that married people can share for a lifetime. It can be hot and nearly overwhelming, or it can be slow and tender. And, believe me, both ways are wonderful."

She grinned at Mary and wagged her eyebrows. But Mary didn't laugh, she looked even more nervous. Rosie sighed and her face sobered. "It's the very best way to express love, but so many people get hung up on it, they don't let themselves enjoy it. Don't be afraid to talk with Bradley about it."

"But, you know, he's experienced," she said. "And...well...I'm not."

"And he's going to be even more nervous because of that," Rosie said.

"Really?"

She nodded. "Yes, because he'll want to be sure it's wonderful, for both of you."

Sighing, Mary looked away for a moment, and then turned back. "I know I'm not...you know...competing with Jeannine. But they were married for so long. What if...?"

Rosie held her hand up and stopped her. "Sex is unique for every couple. Bradley's experience with you will not be like his experience with Jeannine. And because it's unique, he'll be learning too. You both need to find out what works best for both of you."

"How do we do that?"

"You talk to each other," she said. "You let him know what feels good and he does the same."

Mary sat up straight and stared at Rosie. "Really, we're going to have a conversation while we're..." She broke off and her face turned red again.

Laughing, she shook her head. "Sweetie, I don't think it's going to be a conversation," she said. "But you'll be making sounds that he'll understand and he'll do the same."

Mary tucked in the edge of her towel more securely and stood up. "Rosie, I think I'm even more confused," she said.

"Trust me," Rosie said. "Everything will be just wonderful and it will be worth the wait."

Chapter Forty-one

"Rosie, just in time," Stanley said, opening the door to his home even wider. "Please come in."

She walked in, sliding off her coat, but froze in place after a few steps. "Stanley, what have you done to your home?" she asked.

The living room was totally different from the room she had seen only a few days earlier. Instead of a room and furnishings that looked over a decade old, the entire room had been remodeled. Soft warm colors on the wall and rugs, complemented leather furniture and oak tables with splashes of bright complementary colors in toss pillows and art.

"This looks like a room from out of a magazine," she said.

"Well, I ain't saying it does and I ain't saying it don't," he said. "But I do think it looks a mite better in here, myself."

She turned back to face him. "How did you get it all done so fast?" she asked.

He shrugged. "Called in a favor from Cal over at Rite-Way Furniture," he said. "He's got those interior decorator gals that work for him. They came over and lickity-split the whole room looked different."

Walking over to her, he helped her take her coat off the rest of the way. After laying it over the back of the couch, he turned to her and took her hands in his. "They said you'd like it," he said. "Do you? Do you like it Rosie?"

Smiling up at him, she stepped forward and kissed him. "Stanley, I love it," she said. "I really love it."

He breathed an audible sound of relief. "Well, that's good," he said. "'Cause I really did want to make you happy."

He kissed her and held her in his arms. "Rosie, I think I understand most of what Verna wanted," he said. "I still don't remember everything, but one thing I do know, she wanted you to understand who she was and what our life was like afore she died."

Rosie smiled up at him. "I would love to learn more about you and Verna," she said.

He led her to the small dining room and pulled out a chair for her. "I made us supper," he said. "I haven't cooked for a while. But I think it's good."

"I'm sure I will enjoy it," she replied.

"Okay, well, then I'll be right back," he said, hurrying to the kitchen.

Lying on the table, near her plate, was an old leather-bound photo album. Rosie pulled it closer, opened the first page and saw a black and white wedding photo. Although it was over fifty years old, she instantly recognized Stanley and smiled. *What a hunk*, she thought.

She looked at Verna, a petite woman with dark hair and sparkling eyes. She was sporting a bouffant hairstyle and her wedding dress was fitted through her bodice and then full skirted below, a very typical '50s style. Stanley, with a full head of hair, was wearing a black fedora, along with a tuxedo and a black bow tie. *Well, aren't you all Frank Sinatra.*

Smiling, she turned to the next page. Stanley and Verna were standing in front of this house when they first bought it, clutching the "SOLD" sign in their hands. Verna was wearing a dress that looked like it stepped out of a Donna Reed rerun, but she looked perfect in it. *Pearls and high heels*, she thought. *How in the world did she ever get anything done dressed like that?*

The next page showed a smiling Verna holding up a tiny pair of crocheted baby booties. The next page started a collection of smaller photographs attached with Scotch tape and small black corner holders. From the first day of school to Thanksgiving dinner to Christmas morning, the photos were a wonderful history of Stanley's first marriage.

"I didn't mean to take so long," Stanley's apology came from the dining room doorway. "These dang potatoes just wouldn't mash properly."

He carried in a bowl of slightly runny, lumpy mashed potatoes and placed them in the middle of the table.

"They look delicious," Rosie said, closing the album and sliding it back in place.

Stanley pulled out the chair next to her and took her hands in his. "I know this dinner ain't gonna be as good as what you can make," he said. "But I wanted to make dinner for you, you know, to maybe show you how much I appreciate all you do for me."

Leaning forward, she kissed him. "Thank you, Stanley," she said. "I have a feeling that this is going to be the best dinner I've ever eaten."

Nodding, he didn't say a word, just stood up and walked out of the room. In a moment he was carrying a platter with meat loaf covered with ketchup and surrounded with green beans. "I saw on one of those cooking shows how you're supposed to put the food on plate and make it look fancy," he said. "So, I thought I'd try it with the green beans, 'cepting I think the juice is getting the meat a mite soggy."

Rosie bit back a smile and inhaled deeply. "Oh, it smells just delicious."

Stanley filled her plate with about twice of what she usually ate and sat across from her, waiting anxiously for her to take her first bite.

She lifted a forkful of meatloaf. It had a very strong flavor of oregano and she thought she might have chewed on a piece of eggshell, but overall it wasn't bad at all. She smiled up at him. "This is very good," she said. "It has a slight oregano taste."

Grinning and nodding, he leaned forward. "Yeah, the cookbook only said two tablespoons," he said. "But I remember little green flecks being all throughout Verna's meatloaf, so I added a cup of them. Thought it would taste better that way."

Rosie thought Verna's meatloaf must have included parsley, but she wasn't going to say a word against the love-inspired meal. The potatoes were runny and the green beans were cold, but she loved every bite.

"Well, it weren't the best meal I ever ate," Stanley admitted.

Looking up from her empty plate, she shook her head. "Well, that's funny, because it was certainly the best meal I ever ate," she said. "And the love put into it made it even better."

He shrugged, but his face glowed with pleasure. "Thank you, Rosie," he said, leaning over and kissing her.

She wrapped her arms around his neck and kissed him back. "No, thank you, Stanley," she said. "This was perfect."

A moment later, Stanley pushed the dishes to the side and picked up the album. "I wanted to show you this," he explained. "I guess I wanted you to know a little bit about where I come from."

She placed her hands on the top of the album. "While you were in the kitchen I looked through it," she said. "I hope you don't mind."

"No, but you didn't mind?" he asked. "I mean, this don't really have a lot to do with you and me."

"Of course it does," she replied. "This is your family, Stanley. These are your memories and they look like wonderful ones. I loved the photos of Christmas morning and all of the clever things Verna did for birthdays. She was a very creative woman."

"You don't mind?" he asked. "You ain't jealous?"

She shook her head and sighed. "Stanley, I think I would have liked Verna if I had the chance to know her," she said. "She seemed to have a wonderful sense of humor, she raised delightful children and she left you willing to love again, after she was gone. I think that's fairly remarkable."

Stanley looked down at the table for a moment, and then he met Rosie's eyes. "I still can't for the life of me remember what she wanted," he said. "But I did clean up my office."

"Well, if it's important, you'll remember," she said. "Now, kiss me goodbye, so I can go home, get my beauty sleep and be ready for our wedding day."

He leaned forward again and kissed her. "You don't need no beauty sleep," he said. "You're already the most beautiful woman in the world."

"Oh, Stanley," she sighed. "You say the nicest things."

Chapter Forty-two

Clarissa waited for her mother to come home. She had exciting news; she was going to be part of the spelling bee. It was going to be held the following week at school and she hoped her mother would be able to change her shift and see her spell on the stage. She'd been practicing all afternoon.

"Laughter. L-A-U-G-H-T-E-R," she said and then she giggled. "Laughter."

When she heard the lock rattle, she ran toward the door but stopped a few feet away when she saw her mother enter. Becca looked exhausted, her face was pale with a bluish tinge and there were dark circles under her eyes. Her breathing was labored and she fell against the wall once she closed and locked the door.

"Mommy, are you okay?" Clarissa asked, slowly coming forward.

Becca looked up, surprised. "Oh, darling, I didn't see you," she said slowly, trying to hide her heavy breathing. "I had such a busy day, I guess I'm more tired than I thought."

Clarissa put her arms around her mother's waist and guided her to the couch. "Sit down, Mommy; I have some exciting news for you."

Becca let her daughter lead her across the room, grateful for the support. She had felt light-headed all day; barely being able to catch her breath and her medicine did not seem to be working. She sat on the couch and Clarissa snuggled up next to her. "Guess what, Mommy," she said. "There's going to be a spelling bee at school next week and I get to be in it."

Becca laid her head against her daughter's and closed her eyes for a moment. "I'm so proud of you, dear," she said. "But I'm afraid you are going to have to miss it."

Clarissa sat up and pulled away slightly. "Why? I worked really hard. I know my words really well."

"Darling, you aren't going to be attending that school anymore," Becca explained. "You don't even have to go to school tomorrow."

"Why?"

"Because tomorrow, as soon as I get off work and get paid, we are going to the bus station and we are going to take the bus all the way to Florida."

"But why are we going to Florida?" Clarissa asked, trying to keep the panic out of her voice. "Daddy's angels won't be able to find us if we go to Florida."

Becca pulled Clarissa back into her embrace and rocked her for a few moments. "Darling, I'm so sorry," she whispered into her hair. "I know you worked hard on your spelling. And I know you've been such a good girl. But the bad man won't find us if we go far away, to a place like Florida. And I think

I would get better there. It's warmer, so it would be easier for me to breathe."

"But what about Daddy's angels?" she asked.

Becca kissed the top of Clarissa's head. "Oh, any angels sent by your daddy will be able to find us no matter where we go."

"So, I can't go back to my school and say goodbye to my teacher and my friends?"

"No, darling, you just stay home in the morning and then we can sneak away before anyone knows we're gone," she said. "The less people know, the better."

Later that night Clarissa sat next to the window in her bedroom. The neon sign from the bar below was shining brightly and the scantily clad angel was flapping her wings. Clarissa searched in vain for the angel her daddy was going to send, but finally, she gave up and knelt next to her bed. She folded her arms and bent her head. "Dear God, this is Clarissa. Mommy says we are moving tomorrow, but my daddy might not know about it. Please tell him we are going to Florida, 'cause it's warm and Mommy can breathe better. Tell Daddy to please send angels to Florida to take care of us there. And tell him I miss him. Amen."

She climbed up into her bed and pulled the covers up. The apartment was silent for a moment, and then the coughing started again. She quickly slipped from her bed and knelt down again. "And please God, help Mommy to stop coughing. Amen."

Chapter Forty-three

The night sky was so clear you could see the Milky Way from the top of Flagstaff hill in Krape Park. Bradley and Mary sat wrapped in a wool blanket on the top of the picnic bench that overlooked the park and stared up into the sky. "This is so beautiful," Mary said. "I feel like I can reach out and touch them."

Bradley wrapped his arm around her and pulled her even closer. "We could go home where it's warm and watch this on the Internet."

Mary elbowed him and shook her head. "The Internet is not romantic."

"Oh," he replied, nibbling on her ear. "I didn't realize you wanted romantic."

She shivered. "Stop it," she laughed. "That tickles."

He moved back. "It was supposed to be sexy."

"Oh," she said, immediately contrite. "I didn't know that. Go ahead, try again. I'll do better this time."

She heard him snort and his body shook with laughter. "What?"

He shook his head. "Nothing," he laughed.

"I said I'd do better," she said with a huff. "So do it again."

Still laughing he pulled her onto his lap and wrapped the blanket around them tightly, and then he trailed a number of light kisses on her jawline. She shivered again, but this time it definitely did not tickle. She closed her eyes and arched her neck and he kissed along her collarbone and the inside of her neck. Her body grew warmer. "Oh, that's so nice," she whispered as he kissed the corner of her lips. He lifted his head and waited until she opened her eyes. Then he lowered his face to hers and crushed his lips against hers. She moaned softly and then she froze.

Bradley lifted his head. "What's wrong?"

Her eyes, wide with wonder, met his. "This is what Rosie meant," she said.

"What?"

"When Rosie and I were talking about sex, she told me that we would be able to communicate without words," she said, her voice animated and her eyes sparkling with understanding. "We just did that, we just communicated without words."

Rolling his eyes, Bradley pulled her back into his arms. "Well, let's just continue our conversation, shall we?"

She chuckled and nodded. "Oh, of course," she agreed, wrapping her arms around his neck and positioning herself for a fresh round of kisses.

Just before their lips met, Bradley's phone began to ring. He sat back and sighed. "It's the department," he said. "I have to…"

She nodded with understanding.

"Alden," he said into the phone. "Really? Already? And what did they decide?"

He paused for a moment and nodded. "Thank you so much. Yes, I'll tell Mary. Thanks again."

He hung up the phone and kissed Mary with extra enthusiasm.

"What?" she asked, when she could speak again.

"The jury reached a verdict: guilty of manslaughter," he said. "The sentencing will be tomorrow."

"Only manslaughter?" Mary asked. "Why not first degree murder?"

"The jury didn't believe he intended to kill his wife, they believe he thought she was dead and acted to save their baby," he said.

"And Jeannine?" she asked.

"He didn't inject the drug," he said with a shrug. "So they didn't find him culpable."

"How do you feel?" she asked.

He smiled. "Good," he said. "I feel good. I think the judge will send him away for a long time. I feel that justice has been served. How do you feel?"

Taking a deep breath, she smiled back at him. "Relieved," she replied. "Gary Copper is going away and I don't ever have to worry about him again. Now we can concentrate on finding Clarissa."

Bradley stood up, with Mary in his arms and kissed her again. Then he lowered her to the ground. "Come on," he said. "Let's go tell Ian the good news.

And then you can tell me more about this conversation you and Rosie had."

Chapter Forty-four

Rosie stood in front of the mirror in a small room at the church. Mary stood behind her, helping to place hairpins in her hair to hold the veil in place. "Okay, I think it's good," Mary said through a mouthful of bobby pins. "What do you think?"

Rosie turned her head to one side and then to the other and nodded. "Oh Mary, I think it looks perfect."

Mary stood back and looked at her friend. She was dressed in an ivory brocade suit with pearl buttons and four-inch ivory heels. Her veil was a vintage birdcage with a cluster of ivory roses, green shamrocks and black feathers. "You look so beautiful," Mary said, tears filling her eyes. "Stanley is going to be knocked off his feet."

Rosie smiled back at her. "Don't start crying or I'll ruin my mascara and my wedding pictures will look horrid."

Mary laughed, grabbed a tissue and blotted her eyes. "Okay, I'm better now," she said. "So, have you got something old, something new, something borrowed and something blue?"

Rosie nodded. "Let's see, something new is this wonderful suit," she said, twirling in front of the mirror. "Even though it cost me a fortune."

"It was worth every penny," Mary said.

"And something borrowed is my veil," she said. "It belonged to my mother, I just updated it a little."

"Perfect," Mary agreed.

"And, something blue," she said, as she lifted her skirt slightly and with a saucy wink exposed a blue garter on her thigh. "How's this?"

"Well, you have it all covered except something old," Mary said.

Rosie shrugged. "Well, I figured the something old would be me."

Mary rushed forward and threw her arms around Rosie. "You are not old, you are amazing," she said. "And I am so happy for you."

Rosie returned the hug. "Thank you, sweetie, I am so happy," she admitted. "I never thought I would find someone like Stanley."

Laughing, Mary stepped back. "Oh, Rosie, there is no one like Stanley."

Rosie giggled. "I suppose you're right," she said.

A knock on the door interrupted their conversation. "Is the bride ready?" Ian asked from the other side of the door.

Mary turned to Rosie. "Ready?"

Rosie nodded. "As ready as I'll ever be."

Mary opened the door and Ian, dressed in a black tuxedo, walked in. "Wow, you look gorgeous," he said, kissing Rosie on the cheek and lowering his voice. "We can still run away together if you'd like."

She kissed him back and laughed. "And just what would you do if I said yes?" she asked.

"Ah, darling, I'd be the happiest of men for the rest of my life," he said, placing his hand over his heart.

"You flatterer," she said. "But no, I have my mind made up. I'm marrying Stanley today."

"Well then, if your mind is made up, the least I can do is walk you down the aisle," he said, extending his arm. "Are you ready, milady?"

"Yes, I'm ready," Rosie agreed, slipping her arm through his.

"Just wait here," Mary said, slipping out the door. "Let me make sure everything is ready."

Mary hurried down the hall and into the front foyer of the church.

Stanley stood at the front of the church loosening his collar. "Don't know why they insist we dress up like monkeys," he grumbled. "Don't know who thought of ties anywho."

Bradley grinned and leaned over to Stanley. "Stop fussing, everyone will think you're nervous," he said.

Stanley straightened. "Ain't nervous," he said. "Perfectly calm. I ain't no wet-behind-the-ears kid. I know what marriage is all about."

Bradley nodded. "Something old, something new, something borrowed, something blue."

"That's nothing but female stuff," Stanley scoffed. "Superstitious female…"

He paused and his jaw dropped. "Well, I'll be," he said.

"What?" Bradley asked.

"I just remembered," he said, turning to Bradley. "I can't believe it took me this long."

"Took you this long for what?" Bradley asked.

Stanley unpinned his boutonniere and handed it to Bradley. "Hold this for me, okay?" he asked. "I gotta go do something."

Stanley walked past him to the side door in the chapel.

"Wait, Stanley, what am I supposed to tell Rosie?" Bradley called after him.

"Tell her I remembered what Verna wanted," he said. "Tell her I love her."

Chapter Forty-five

The courtroom was nearly deserted on the late Friday afternoon, especially since it was St. Patrick's Day and many had taken part in the parade and after work celebrations. Gary Copper was escorted into the antechamber, handcuffs on his wrists and shackles on his legs, wearing an orange jumpsuit.

"Really, is this necessary?" Greg Thanner asked. "I insist you remove these restraining implements from his person. He is remanded to my custody while he is in the courtroom with me, I will be responsible for him."

"I'm sorry, Mr. Thanner, but security requires…" the first officer began.

"Excuse me, but do you want to be a part of the countersuit we are leveling against this county?" he asked. "Either you take off these handcuffs and shackles, or you will see us in court."

The officers looked at each other and shrugged. "We'll be right outside the door, waiting," the first one said, and he bent and removed the security apparatus.

Once the door had closed, Thanner sat in a chair across from Gary Copper. Gary shook his head. "I am disappointed in you, Greg," Gary began. "You were supposed to get me off. And yet, here I am, convicted of manslaughter. What did I pay you for?"

Thanner wiped a handkerchief over his moist forehead. "I did the best I could," he defended. "Once you told them about cutting into your wife, my hands were tied."

Gary sat back in his chair. "Oh, so this is my fault?" he asked. "You were the one who suggested I testify on my own behalf."

Thanner nodded his head. "Well, I admit that was a misjudgment on my part."

Gary smiled. "They say confession is good for the soul," he said. "Especially a confession just before you die."

The officers on the other side of the door heard a muffled noise and looked at each other. But the noise wasn't repeated, so they simply shrugged and waited for Thanner to notify them he was ready to bring Gary into the courtroom.

Chapter Forty-six

It was starting to get dark; Clarissa watched the streetlights turn on and watched the grocery store slide the metal grate over its windows and close up for the day. She scanned the streets from the living room window, waiting for her mother.

She had packed all of her clothes and her few belongings into her backpack. That morning her mother had suggested that she also carry all of their money in her backpack, because it would be a lesser target for pickpockets than her mother's purse. But that was early in the morning and her mother was supposed to have been home by lunchtime.

She walked into her bedroom and looked out her window, down to the bar across the street. Ever since early that afternoon, there had been a steady stream of customers into the bar. They were all wearing green hats or green clothing. Clarissa remembered her teacher telling them about St. Patrick's Day and how all of the students should wear green to school that day. She sighed; she was really going to miss her teacher.

The lock rattled and Clarissa hurried out of her room. Her mother stumbled into the apartment and Clarissa ran forward to catch her. "Sorry, sweetheart," she gasped. "I just need to catch my breath."

Clarissa led her over to the nearest chair and helped her sit down. "Let me get you some water, Mommy," she said. "So you can take your medicine."

Becca smiled at her daughter. "That would be lovely, sunshine, thank you."

Becca listened to Clarissa's footsteps enter the kitchen, and took a napkin from her pocket. The white napkin was already dotted with specks of dried blood. Becca lifted it to her mouth and coughed softly, expelling a little more blood. She quickly wiped her mouth and stuffed the napkin back in her pocket before Clarissa came into the room.

Handing her mother the cup of water, Clarissa looked worried. "Maybe you should rest and we can go tomorrow," she suggested.

Sipping the water, Becca shook her head. "No," she finally said. "This is the perfect day. We can get lost in the St. Patrick's Day crowds and no one will be able to track us."

"Are you sure, Mommy?" Clarissa asked.

Becca nodded and silently prayed for some more strength. "I'm sure, honey."

Chapter Forty-seven

Stanley pushed open his front door and hurried into the house, not even taking the time to close the door behind him. He first went to his bedroom, throwing open the closet and searching the shelves and the boxes on the floor. "Nothing," he muttered.

He walked past his office, knowing what he was looking for was not in there either, since he just spent the past week cleaning it. Moving on to the guest room, he pulled open drawers and examined the closet and under the bed. He was having no luck at all.

Walking through the kitchen, he opened the door to the basement. Glancing quickly, he thought he saw a light down below, but in a moment it was gone. Shrugging, he turned on the basement light and hurried down the narrow steps. Years ago Verna had asked him to create a series of shelving units all along the walls of the basement. The shelves closest to the door held personal items and kitchen equipment. Those across the way were supposed to hold camping equipment and tools. He bit his lip, knowing that he hadn't been as careful in the past few years with putting things were they needed to be. He hoped he could still find it.

Knowing the first unit was filled with Christmas ornaments, he skipped that one. The second unit held all of the canning equipment; it wouldn't be in there either. He moved down to the third shelving unit and found a number of boxes that were labeled in Verna's handwriting. He opened the first one and found it filled with items that belonged to their children; books, toys, sports equipment and miscellaneous trophies filled several shelves worth of boxes.

The last set of shelves had boxes that were haphazardly placed on each level. There were no markings on the box and the lids were fastened with duct tape. He shook his head, these must have been the boxes he put away. He pulled down the first box and ripped open the top. A waft of Verna's perfume filled the air and he quickly looked around, sure that she was standing nearby. He looked down and saw the box held some of the clothes from her closet. He picked up a blue cardigan and stroked it lovingly. It was her favorite sweater; she wore it nearly every day in the winter as she worked around the house. He lifted it to his face and inhaled her perfume as bittersweet memories came flooding into his mind.

"Oh, Verna, am I doing the right thing?" he asked aloud.

"Well, it's a little late to ask that question," Verna's voice came from directly behind Stanley.

He jumped around and started when he saw her, standing just a few feet away. "Verna?"

"You got that sweet woman waiting at the altar for you and now you're going to ask if you should be marrying her?" she asked, shaking her finger at him. "Why, Stanley Wagner, what kind of man are you anyway?"

"I guess I'm the confused kind, Verna," he said. "How come you're back here, messing around with my mind?"

"Because, if I hadn't come back, you would have forgotten," she said. "And I didn't want you to forget."

Stanley looked away for a moment. "Pert near forgot, until I was standing at the altar, waiting for the music to begin," he said. "So, I rushed home to find it."

She smiled at him. "Do you love her?" she asked.

"I won't be hurting your feelings iffen I tell you the truth?" he asked.

"Tell me the truth, Stanley."

"I love her," he said. "It don't take away from the love I felt for you. It's different, but it's right."

"I know it's right," she said. "I like her, Stanley."

He smiled. "I'm glad you do," he said. "She said she thought she'd like you too."

"Well, then, since you've got that settled, I'll just be on my way," she said, and she started fading away.

"Wait! Verna! I can't find it," he said. "I'm keeping her waiting and I can't find it."

Verna was nearly gone, but he heard her whisper into his ear. "Check in the pocket of my favorite sweater, Stanley."

He turned the sweater around and put his hand in the right front pocket. All that was inside was a folded tissue. Then he put his hand into the left pocket and a smile spread over his face. "Thank you, Verna."

Chapter Forty-eight

"Tell me again what he said when he left?" Rosie asked Bradley, as she blotted her eyes with a lace handkerchief.

They were all standing inside the small room Rosie had used to get dressed. Bradley had informed the minister things were going to be a little later than expected and then he found Mary in the lobby. Together they broke the news to Rosie.

"He just said he remembered what Verna wanted and that he loved you," Bradley repeated. "I'm sorry, Rosie, I don't know what's going on."

Mary wrapped her arms around Rosie. "I'm sure there's a good explanation," she said. "I'm sure that he will be back in just a few minutes."

Rosie sniffed. "He's been gone for fifteen minutes," she said, her voice quivering. "The poor organist is running out of music. I don't know what I'm going to do."

"Darling, what you're going to do is have faith in the man you love," Ian said.

Rosie turned and looked at him. "But he left…"

Ian shook his head. "Rosie, you know that Stanley and I rarely see eye to eye, but I will tell you one thing I know, Stanley is a man of honor. He would not leave you stranded at the altar. If he's gone, it's for a damn good reason."

Stanley cleared his throat as he stood in the doorway of the room and they all turned around. "I thank you, Ian," he said. "I thought it was important, or I wouldn't have left, I swear Rosie."

"What was it?" she asked.

"I've got something for you, Rosie," he said, walking toward her, "something that Verna wanted me to remember."

"Would you both like a moment alone?" Ian asked.

Stanley nodded. "Yeah, that'd be nice."

Once they left the room, Stanley reached into his pocket and pulled out a strand of pearls.

"Oh, Stanley, they are beautiful," Rosie said.

"These pearls belonged to my great-grandmother. They've been passed down to new brides through every generation," Stanley explained. "Verna got them on our wedding day."

Rosie stepped back. "But these belong to her, or to one of your children," she said.

He shook his head. "When Verna was sick, she told me that someday I would find someone special. Someone I could love again, with all my heart. She told me she wanted her to have these pearls," he explained. "That's what she wanted me to remember. She wanted you to have these."

He moved behind her, laid the pearls over her neck and fastened the clasp. Then he pressed a kiss on the back of her neck. "I love you, Rosie," he said.

She turned and wrapped her arms around his neck. "And I love you too Stanley," she whispered, her voice overcome with emotion. "Let's get married."

He smiled and kissed her one more time. "That's the best idea I've heard all day."

Chapter Forty-nine

The bus station was enormous. *E-N-O-R-M-O-U-S*, Clarissa thought. There had to be hundreds of people running back and forth, rushing to catch their bus. Although everyone seemed to be in a very friendly mood – laughing and patting each other on the back. Clarissa decided she liked St. Patrick's Day.

They had taken a city bus to the subway station and taken the subway train to downtown and then walked six blocks to the bus station. Clarissa's feet hurt and she was hungry and tired. She thought about the food they left in their refrigerator in the apartment and her stomach growled. Her mother told her they were playing a game. They were going to make people think something happened to them, like they died and disappeared. That way, the bad man would stop looking for them. So, they left some of their clothes and all of their food and locked up the apartment like they were planning on coming back.

The big clock at the end of the terminal said it was eight o'clock. Clarissa knew their bus to Florida didn't leave until two o'clock in the morning, so they had to stay in the station for six hours. Clarissa hoped there was something to eat at the station.

"Come on, sweetheart," Becca said. "Let's go sit down on those benches over there."

Most of the wooden benches in the middle of the station were empty. Becca led Clarissa over to a bench near the ticket booth and they piled their belongings next to them and sat down.

"Mommy, can we get something to eat?" she asked. "I'm a little bit hungry."

Becca reached into her purse and pulled out a small package of Saltine crackers. "Here, darling, why don't you eat these," she said. "Then you should take a nap. We can buy some food when we get closer to Florida."

Clarissa opened the cellophane wrapper and pulled the two crackers out. She took tiny bites, eating around the edges of the crackers to make them last longer. But in a few minutes they were gone and her stomach still felt empty.

Becca placed her arm around Clarissa and pulled her close. "Now, get some rest, sweetheart," she whispered. "Two o'clock isn't for a very long time."

Clarissa cuddled close to her mother, placed her head on her lap and drifted to sleep. In the back of her mind she could hear her mother's occasional cough and the familiar sound was actually soothing.

Becca stroked her daughter's hair and tried to force oxygen into her lungs. The last couple of blocks had been so hard, she thought she was going faint a number of times. But somehow they made it and soon they would be safe.

She slowly looked around the bus station. Ever since they left their apartment, she had the

287

feeling someone was watching them. She decided to take the less direct route, just to throw anyone off their path. But even now, she didn't feel safe.

She coughed again and lifted her hand to wipe away the moisture on her lips. Her heart dropped when she saw her hand was covered with blood. She reached into her purse once again, pulled out her plastic bag of pills and swallowed two of them. *That should do the trick*, she thought. *If one is good, two must be better.*

Chapter Fifty

The newlyweds were happily moving from one table to the next, greeting friends and taking photos.

"They look so great," Mary said, glancing at them as she and Bradley spun slowly around the dance floor.

"Yeah, there were a couple of minutes there when I didn't know what was going to happen," Bradley admitted.

Mary grinned. "You mean when Stanley forgot he was supposed to say, 'I do?'" she asked.

Laughing, he nodded. "Well, that one too," he acknowledged. "But all it took was a slight elbow from his best man…"

"You were amazing," Mary said, reaching up and placing a kiss on his cheek.

"It's nice to feel like everything's getting back to normal," he said. "The trial is finally over and Rosie and Stanley are married."

"And with Copper in prison, maybe Becca will feel like she can return to Freeport with Clarissa," Mary suggested.

"Yeah, well, that's next on our agenda," he said. "We need to go into Chicago and find her."

The music stopped and Bradley led her back toward their table. "I got a call from Bernie," he said.

"He said his daughter is following up on some leads. They think they might have found someone, a gypsy, who's seen Clarissa."

"Oh, that's wonderful," Mary said. "We can drive in tomorrow."

Bradley pulled out Mary's chair for her and was about to sit down when his phone rang. "Alden," he answered, then his face turned pale and he slowly took his seat. "Why was he allowed out of his restraints? When did they discover he was gone? Well, hell, he's got a half day's lead on us."

Mary put her hand on Bradley's arm, her blood turning cold. He turned to her, his face grave and nodded. "Copper has escaped and Thanner is dead."

Chapter Fifty-one

Clarissa woke up from her nap and looked around in confusion. Suddenly she remembered they were in the bus station. She turned to her mother, but her mother's eyes were closed. Clarissa smiled, she must be sleeping too. Remembering how frequently her mother had been coughing just before she fell asleep, she was happy to see that she was finally resting peacefully.

She looked up at the clock and saw that it was almost midnight. Her daddy used to tell her that was the magic time. Clarissa wondered if she would see any magic in the bus station. She looked around and saw some people watching her. She pulled her backpack closer to her and slipped her arm through the strap. She didn't want anyone to take their money. It was her job to keep it safe.

Her stomach growled again. She wondered if her mother had any more crackers in her purse. Keeping one arm firmly around her backpack, she reached over to the purse situated between her mother and the end of the bench. Her mother's arm was slung through the handle to protect it, just like Clarissa was doing with her backpack.

She peeked up at her mother. Her eyes were still closed and Clarissa didn't want to wake her. Carefully, she lifted her mother's arm up and slid the purse handle forward, so she could reach inside. But the purse was hanging off the side of the bench and it started to slip to the ground. As she grabbed for the purse, the backpack swung around and bounced against her mother.

Immediately regretful, she pushed the purse back in place and turned to apologize for waking her up. But when she turned, her mother's eyes were still closed.

Clarissa sat up on the bench, her heart pounding against her chest. She lifted her mother's arm, the one that had been around her shoulders, and let it go. It dropped with a thud against the bench and her mother's eyes still did not open.

"Mommy?" she whispered. "Mommy, it's time to wake up."

Her mother still didn't move.

Clarissa looked around; no one seemed to be watching them. She sat up on her knees and placed her face against her mother's cheek. *Please breathe, Mommy*, she prayed. *Please breathe.*

But as soon as she felt her mother's cold, stiff cheek, she knew the truth. Her mother was dead.

She buried her face against her mother's neck, as she wept soundlessly. *What can I do now? Where am I supposed to go? Why aren't there any angels?*

A noise startled her and she turned around. The man that stood in front of the bench just stared at her for a moment. Then he looked beyond her and studied her mother for a moment. Finally, he smiled and squatted down, so he could see her face. "Hello Clarissa," he said. "It's so nice to finally meet you."

Clarissa scooted back on the bench, as close to her mother as possible. She wiped the tears from her eyes and took a deep breath. Maybe the man couldn't tell her mother was dead. Maybe he wouldn't realize her mother was dead. "My mom's just asleep," she lied, "so…no one better think about taking anything."

"You've had a pretty rough day, kid, haven't you?" the man asked, then he shook his head. "Let's be real, you've had a pretty rough life."

Looking around at the bus station, it seemed that they were suddenly alone. There was no one around who would come running if she screamed. Clarissa shook her head. "Are you the bad man?" she asked, her voice shaking.

"Oh, no, Clarissa," he replied. "I'm a friend of your dad's. My name is Mike, and I'm your guardian angel."

About the author:

Terri Reid lives near Freeport, the home of the Mary O'Reilly Mystery Series, and loves a good ghost story. She lives in a hundred-year-old farmhouse complete with its own ghost. She loves hearing from her readers at author@terrireid.com.

Books by Terri Reid:

Loose Ends – A Mary O'Reilly Paranormal Mystery (Book One)

Good Tidings – A Mary O'Reilly Paranormal Mystery (Book Two)

Never Forgotten – A Mary O'Reilly Paranormal Mystery (Book Three)

Final Call – A Mary O'Reilly Paranormal Mystery (Book Four)

Darkness Exposed – A Mary O'Reilly Paranormal Mystery (Book Five)

Natural Reaction – A Mary O'Reilly Paranormal Mystery (Book Six)

Secret Hollows – A Mary O'Reilly Paranormal Mystery (Book Seven)

Broken Promises – A Mary O'Reilly Paranormal Mystery (Book Eight)

Twisted Paths – A Mary O'Reilly Paranormal Mystery (Book Nine)

Veiled Passages – A Mary O'Reilly Paranormal Mystery (Book Ten)

Bumpy Roads – A Mary O'Reilly Paranormal Mystery (Book Eleven)

The Ghosts Of New Orleans – A Paranormal
Research and Containment Division (PRCD) Case
File

5526306R00162

Made in the USA
San Bernardino, CA
10 November 2013